HITTAZ 2

Real Killaz Don't Miss

LOU GARDEN PRICE, SR.

URBAN AINT DEAD PRESENTS

CONTENTS

URBAN AINT DEAD

Contact Author at: paralegal.louprice@gmail.com (for book editing, ghostwriting quotes).

Snail mail: LOU GARDEN PRICE SBI 00454309

Delaware DOC 1101

PO Box 96777

Las Vegas Nevada 89193

**See: GettingOut.com/create account

Search Lou Garden Price SBI #00454309

James T Vaughn Correctional Center, Smyrna DELAWARE

For tablet connection. Download the gettingout.com app.

Contact Publisher at www.urbanaintdead.com

Email: urbanaintdead@gmail.com

Print ISBN: 979-8-9869098-0-6

Ebook ISBN: 979-8-9869098-1-3

URBAN AINT DEAD

Like our page on Facebook Page:

www.facebook.com/urbanaintdead

&

Follow us on Instagram:

@urbanaintdead

SUBMISSION GUIDELINES

Submit the first three chapters of your completed manuscript to urbanaintdead@gmail.com, subject line: Your book's title. The manuscript must be in a .doc file and sent as an attachment. The document should be in Times New Roman, double-spaced and in size 12 font. Also, provide your synopsis and full contact information. If sending multiple submissions, they must each be in a separate email.

Have a story but no way to submit it electronically? You can still submit to URBAN AINT DEAD. Send in the first three chapters, written or typed, of your completed manuscript to:

URBAN AINT DEAD

P.O Box 960780

Riverdale GA., 30296

DO NOT send original manuscript. Must be a duplicate.

Provide your synopsis and a cover letter containing your full contact information

Thanks for considering URBAN AINT DEAD

INTRODUCTION

Elijah R. Freeman

The first time I read a story by Lou it was a submission he'd made to us that made it past our Beta Readers. The book was titled SOSAFROMSCARFACE. I had endured a long two weeks of dreadful manuscripts, and I remember thinking to myself, "another one." I was not looking forward to reading it. I let it sit in my inbox a couple days as I busied myself with U.A.D business and I remember seeing it every so often when I perused through the company email and my next fleeting thought was "Sosa From Scarface? Who does this guy think he is?"

The following day I opened it and realized that he had sent the full manuscript instead of the required three chapters. It usually takes me a chapter to a chapter and a half to decide if an author is a fit for the company, but by the time I made it to chapter seven I realized that not only was he a fit, Lou Garden Price, Sr. was an Urban Fiction genius!

When I first discovered Urban Fiction/Street Lit literally everything HIT! Years passed, the market became saturated with bullshit authors that gave the black eye and before I knew it I was in the hole listening to niggas refuse to trade books with other inmates because the book was Urban.

Being an Urban Fiction author myself with four books on the market at the time, it made me feel some type of way. It wasn't I book I penned personally that had been refused but having a genuine love for the genre, that struck a nerve. I began plotting on a new era in Urban Fiction, and URBAN AINT DEAD was born.

Lou's meticulous story telling is everything I envisioned and more. It has that throwback Street Lit vibe with a new feel. Eccentric plotlines that highlight the brilliance of his imagination without leaving the bounds of fictional realism. His prose is credible, his characters are 3-Demensional, and his pen will leave you wanting more.

If you thought Hittaz 1 was poppin', part 2 is about to rock your world. Grab yo strap and vest up.

Real killaz don't miss...

CHAPTER ONE

The Paper Place #2
New Rochelle, NY
8:00 AM Friday

Rising at 4:00 AM, he sent a simple text message to his cousin D'Mira.

Joke: Meet me by yourself at the New Rochelle Metro-North train station at 8:00 AM. Sent Uber to arrive at 6:00 AM. Put $300 in your *Cash App* to pay moms for babysitting, etc. Don't say nothin' to nobody. Time to repay your love and loyalty to me.

At 5:45 AM, D'Mira returned the text.

Mira: Almost out the door. Hope I don't have to be dressed a certain type of way??

Joke: Nah, you good. Just come presentable like if you going to a bank, real estate broker, or somethin'...

D'Mira arrived at the Metro-North train station by 7:25 AM and Joker was already there waiting. He observed closely as the

Uber driver pulled off and he checked left and right in every direction to see if she had been followed before driving up to where she stood out front of the train station. At first glance, she did not know that it was Joker pulling up in the opulent new Cadillac SUV.

"Red!" She shrieked when the window came down.

"Get in," he beckoned to the plain-looking, brown skinned young woman and she walked around and got in on the passenger side. "How was the ride up?"

"Not bad," She said as she leaned over to kiss his right cheek. "Hot ride, cuz!"

"What up wit it?" He asked her.

"Everything's, everything."

"EIE," he nodded. He drove up to North Avenue and explained everything to her. "I'm settin' you up in your own TPP branch."

"TPP?"

"The Paper Place," he said. "We have a large store up in Rockland County named the same. I'll have my wife and a few of my girls help you establish the store and hire a staff to run it. We already got you the lease, bought and paid for the year. And directly across the street is another store/office space. Upstairs from that space are newly renovated apartments."

"What's the second store space for? And how many apartments are up there?"

"Four," he replied. "All are different sizes but the rooms are pretty spacious. A two bedroom, a three bedroom, and two four bedroom apartments and a large parking area in the rear. I want you to move Auntie Minnie and the kids into the two four bedrooms. The kids can have rooms in both apartments. C'mon, lemme show you."

He parked out front on Main Street, and after putting money into the parking meter to cover two hours, he speed-walked across the street to *The Paper Place.* The insides of the windows were plastered with bright neon orange paper to block the view of anyone who tried to look inside.

The front door was open and there were six Mexican men and two Mexican women inside completing final renovation work. Joker explained that he had hired the immigrants to cover most of the construction and repair work that needed to be done.

"Meet the Ramirez-Lobo family." Joker introduced them. "Paco."

"Si, Senior, Rojo," the eldest man answered, climbing down off of the ladder holding a power drill in his left hand. "Buenos, dias."

"Good mornin'," Joker replied. "Meet the new manager of The Paper Place, Miss Dukes."

"Senorita," Paco acknowledged her with a head nod. "Mucho, gusto."

"They all stay in the basement," Joker informed her. "There's a shower and kitchen down there so... I heard their story from some other Mexicans I hired up Nyack and it turns out they did contract construction work for the Mexican government in, um, Mexico City?"

"Monterrey," Paco corrected him.

"Monterrey," Joker continued. "Anyhow... they're undocumented but they're real good at what they do. Anything you need fixed, call Paco. They all get ten dollars an hour under the table, forty hours a week, and they stay on-call for overtime."

Leaving out of the store, he continued to speak as they crossed the street. "TPP will be open in a week or two so I need you up here now. If Auntie Minnie so much as breathes one word about stayin' in Brooklyn then let her. I can't trust her."

When they reached the outside door to the other office/space, Mira grabbed his arm to get his attention. "Then let me leave her in Fort Green, Red."

"What about the kids?" He asked. "I'm demandin' a lot from you. You'll be paid a lot..."

"Talk about that," she wanted to know. "What's my salary?"

"Five thousand a month," he told her. "About twelve hundred

fifty a week. Above ground. Your checks will come from TPP, LLC."

"So, I'll hire a sitter," she shrugged. "A nanny to help me full time. Believe me... she's tryna get you locked up. She calls them detectives sayin' what she 'hears' about EIE on the street..."

"So she's tryin' everything," he muttered as he fished the keys out of his pocket. "Did the cops tells her I have a bonafide alibi?"

"Yeah... about you bein' pulled over and in a New Jersey IKEA at the time?"

He let them into the side door entrance which led up a staircase to the apartments above. To the right was an elevator. Across the small lobby were the mailboxes for the four apartments.

"Yeah, that's it."

"They don't trust the alibi," D'Mira informed him. "The one cop, Pope, said to Mama that it was too convenient."

"These are the keys to the entire building," he pointed out to her. "This is ring two... all the keys are numbered. The store keys all look distinguished from the apartment keys. Your other key ring is ring number one. It has less keys on it. This is your fuckin' security. I made you a copy and I have the originals."

He walked with her through the building, starting in the basement. In the laundry room there were four washers and four dryers. Joker shoved her the keys that would open the coin-operated washers and dryers and also the key that would unlock the laundry room door.

They walked past a door with an old padlock on it, prompting her to ask about the room. He opened it with a separate key and pulled open the door. The room was filled to capacity with plywood, sheetrock, boxes of nails, buckets of paint, two-by-fours, and endless other varieties of building materials. There was so much of it there was no way anyone could get to the back of the room. What D'Mira didn't realize was that Joker, under cover of night, had stashed a million dollars in cash inside of a wall he had constructed in the rear of the room.

"These construction supplies we'll use on other sites," he lied to her. "For now, just keep everyone out. And in the future, we may add more supplies, or supply rooms, down here. I'll let you know."

They moved on upstairs after locking the "supply room" back up.

Upstairs, in the first four-bedroom apartment, D'Mira was excited about what she saw. "It's really nice. Cherry wood floors, easy to keep clean with two messy kids... new stove top, new oven, a dishwasher, and that refrigerator is insane!"

"Set yourself up here within seventy-two hours," Joker instructed her. "Get online and get a nanny. Set her up in the four bedroom apartment down the hall. I'm putting the Ramirez-Lobo Family in the other apartments because I have them travelin' up to Nyack for work, too."

"You really trust them?"

"For now I do." He removed an envelope full of money out of his inside coat pocket. "Here's a full-month's advance on your pay."

"What if Mama asks questions?"

Joker looked at her for a second. "You grown... You movin' out. Period. Definitely don't give no indication about what we doin'. Give her five hundred or somethin' and send her off shoppin' all day so she ain't there when you leave. You'll think of something'."

"I'll handle it."

"That's what I need to hear."

A text message came through from Uzenna. He read it immediately.

Wifey: Two detectives from NYPD came to the spot threatening to arrest all of us for ID theft unless I came in to answer questions. I'll be at Nyack Police Department HQ.

"Before you leave..." he continued. "Familiarize yourself with those keys and both properties. Create a 'To Do List' and do it. I expect top performance outta you. So expect to attend certain classes I send you to for real estate, management skills, and such. We doin' some real big things, D, and your salary will increase –

maybe even double. But you'll be sent on flights to look at property, sell property, buy property."

"Double?" She looked surprised and overjoyed. "Thank you for the sixty grand salary... oh my God, Red! I needed somethin' like this!"

"Don't start cryin', babe," he said calmly. "I remember loyalty and never forget betrayal. You got the job but you need to hit the ground runnin'. If you ain't livin' up to it, I'll fire you just as quick."

"You won't ever have to do that."

"Okay," he kissed her cheek. "I gotta go. You got an Uber account?"

"Uber's expensive. No."

Before he left, he set up an Uber account for her on her cellphone. "Movin' forward, try to pay for everything with a debit or credit card. We'll give you a TPP credit card to use for everything related to TPP business. Come tax season, we'll write the majority of those expenses off. Get in the habit of keepin' receipts for all purchases; I don't care if it's only a two dollar cheeseburger."

He went outside and made a telephone call from the driver's seat of his Cadillac truck.

"Atwater, Norris and Montecristo," a cheery female receptionist answered. *"How may I help you?"*

"I need to speak to Mecca Montecristo please," Joker requested. *"I have an emergency. My name is David Hodges."*

"Um, she's on a call right now, can I-?"

Joker cut her off. *"I also have a hundred thousand dollar retainer I can always take somewhere else."*

"Give me a minute to knock on her door," the receptionist said. *"Please hold."*

"I'll hold."

Joker started driving up Main Street towards North Avenue. He was headed up to Nyack to get Uzenna out of the clutches of the NYPD investigators.

"Mr. Hodges?" a different female's voice answered the line this time. *"Mecca Montecristo here."*

"I need you to meet me at the Nyack Police Department Headquarters, like, yesterday," Joker began. *"If you send me your bank's routing number and information, I'll transfer a hundred thousand dollars there right now."*

"I'll text it," she told him. *"Give me your cell."*

He gave her his cellphone number and a moment later, her text came through. He stopped at a gas station and parked next to the bathrooms. He then accessed the WSFS Bank website and logged into the TPP, LLC account. It took barely three minutes to make the electronic transfer to the high-powered female attorney's account.

"Done," he finally told her.

"Wait a moment please," she said slowly. Seconds later, *"Okay. You sure know how to get our attention. I'm assuming you don't want to speak on the phone so I'll meet you at NYPDH in an hour."*

"The clients name is Uzenna Jade Hodges," he said. *"She's my wife. I'll see you there."*

They hung up.

CHAPTER TWO

Westchester County Mall
Yonkers, NY
Friday 3:00 PM

Ghostman Dinero noticed her window shopping outside of the new Gucci store as he just exited Auntie Annie's bakery next door to it. He was doing some clothes and jewelry shopping at the Westchester County Mall when the wonderful aroma of freshly baked sweet pretzels drew him into the famous bakery. And as he came out eating his small purchase, he noticed the lovely young Latina as she examined the expensive designer clothing and handbags being displayed in the store's window.

She had on what appeared to be a catholic school uniform for girls that consisted of an all-white, starched, long sleeved shirt, a gray pleated skirt, a blue sweater, and a black curly tresses. She wore glasses with a silver frame and Ghostman could see that she had a provocatively shaped body and small breasts. Her face was partially covered with a protective mask that had the Dominican flag designed on it.

"Dominicana," he greeted her. "Ola, mi amor."

She looked at him. "Ola."

"I'm Blue Johnson," he introduced himself.

"Bianca Velazquez," she was mildly pleased at what she saw. A tall, well-built, dark skinned man who was not a flashy dresser but a great dresser no less.

"Sorry to bother you," he apologized to her. "But I came out the bakery, saw you.... And was struck in the chest by somethin'."

She turned toward him to get a better look. "What's that mean?"

"It means I see beautiful females all day and I keep it movin'," he explained. "Like, so what? But you're a different matter all together. Sometimes a man just knows to stop... Or miss the best thing to ever cross his path."

That caused her to smile. "You got all that from one look?"

He smiled a mouthful of gold teeth. "Well, you try eatin' a glazed pretzel from Auntie Annie's and see a Dominican angel like you... You'll like her, too."

"I doubt it," she walked away from him. "I don't do females. I go to Saint Joseph's all-girls school. I hate bitches."

Ghostman followed her into the store. "You buyin' or just lookin' around?"

"I wish I was buyin'!" She laughed. "I lost my job at the movie theater to the pandemic and can't find work yet."

"How old are you?"

"Eighteen. I'm a Senior."

He looked at her suspiciously. "Wonder how many high schoolers say they're eighteen when they're really seventeen or sixteen."

She laughed. "You ain't nobody important to lie to."

"You right," he agreed. "What if I have a job for you."

That made her stop and look at him. "Doin' what?"

"I don't know," he joked. "Help me out here. I like you and I'm thinkin' of ways to get you to hang out wit me."

"Why not just say that? How old are you anyway?"

"I'm a grown man, mami. No kids. No wife. I'm almost thirty."

She paused. *He looked really good*, she thought to herself. *He's a damned good dresser.* But being inexperienced with men... she was hesitant.

"It's early in the day," he told her. "Just after three o'clock. How about we hang out? We can listen to the new Trey Songz, some Chris Brown, or Bad Bunny."

"You listen to Bad Bunny?"

"Anuel, Prince Royce, Daddy Yankee, Dan Dmar, and a lot more," he told her. "We can ride and smoke, hit a nice restaurant, whatever. Long as I can hang out with you and get to know you."

"Dressed like this?" She asked. "No way. I'm in this corny uniform... Plus, I was at school all day. I need a bath."

"Where you live?"

"In New Rochelle," she said. "I took the bus here after school. My school is in Hortsdale."

He thought it was over. "Get everything you want from this Gucci store, baby girl. Ain't no time to be goin' to New Rochelle to get ready."

She stared at him blankly. "Get what I want? This is the Gucci store, Blue. I'm not takin' advantage of nobody like that."

He waved her off. "It's nothin', love."

She was adamant. "Nah, man. Let's just hang out. I'll go like this."

"Damn," he said as he took her hand. "I'm feelin' you even more now. I feel like I won the lottery with a bad ass Dominican mami like you. Can we at least buy you somethin' that'll make you feel more comfortable? Let's go to Consuela's Clothing or to that ladies denim store downstairs, Her Jeans."

She thought it through. "You don't have to."

"If it makes you feel better... I don't plan on lettin' you leave my life after tonight. So I'm not just bein' reckless here. And once you get to know me... You won't go nowhere either."

She held onto his hand as they walked into Consuela's where he helped her choose a trendy jacket, turtle neck sweater, and jeans outfit. She accessorized it with a stylish tan hat, Coach bag, and small black leather gloves. He threw several other items into the shopping cart.

She examined them. "Panties, bras... You must be an expert because these are my exact sizes."

"I'm a good guesser," he smiled charmingly at her.

Walking outside of the main entrance to the mall, they were hit by a strong gust of cold air. She squealed out of surprise as he carried all of their bags, trotting toward where he parked at.

"I'm right up here," he told her as they approached the new blue Cadillac truck. He opened it with voice-print command from his iPhone. He had already started it up and had the heat warming up before they had even exited the mall. "Jump on in. It's already warm in there, mami."

"Dios mio," She cooed as she opened the front side passenger door and sat down in the blue leather heated seat. "This is a really nice truck."

He threw their purchases in the rear cargo hold and then joined her up front. She continued to look around the beautiful luxurious interior of the armored truck. She noticed the computers, the multiple TV screens, satellite radio and television controls, and the smooth silence as the car drove along.

"You comfortable, Bianca?" He looked over at her.

She nodded. "I can't get over how nice this thing is. What's that?"

She pointed at a small square digital monitor mounted next to the computer that was custom installed by Cadillac.

"That's actually a police scanner," he informed her. "It has multiple applications that allow me to listen in on different law enforcement agencies. City police, the sheriff department, highway patrol state boys, and whatnot."

"Oh," she said. "You must be a bad boy to need all that."

He filled in no blanks. Instead, he drove up to the Radisson Hotel and she wondered why they had stopped there.

"You look nervous," he smiled at her again. "Don't be."

She looked around. "Well... I see a hotel. I don't... I'm just an eighteen year old high school girl. What do I know? You're a man. A *real* man. So, yeah I'm nervous."

"Calm down, mami," he soothed her. "You've never been with a man before, huhn?"

"Yes I have!" She said quickly. Maybe too quickly. "Well, kinda."

He was suddenly amused by the innocence of the fresh-faced Dominican girl. "Kinda what? You never had a dick before? Cute as you are? You coulda had plenty."

He played music by Trey Songz and rolled up a blunt of purple haze. He had her laughing at herself and her shyness started disappearing little by little.

"I've seen a dick before!" She told him as she exhaled the blunt smoke and started coughing. "I had a boyfriend."

"So, you seen one dick."

She nodded. "But we never... you know!"

"Never what?"

"Never did it."

"Stop the shy stuff. Just say 'he never put it in my pussy'."

"I'm not sayin' that!" She exclaimed, laughing.

"He ever showed you how to suck it?"

She giggled and blushed. "No comment."

He looked at her closely. "Mmm."

"What 'mmm' mean?"

"You're a virgin," he said slowly. "And I can picture you suckin' on what I have. I can imagine that soft, wet, mouth of yours drivin' me up a wall."

"My God!" she murmured, squeezing her white stocking-clad thighs together. "You are so bad!"

"You're the bad one. And I mean bad meanin' *good*. A virgin... Now I definitely better stay outta that hotel. You go in, pay for a room, shower, and dress up. When you're done, just come back down."

Peeling off two $100 bills, he gave them to her. "Keep the change."

"You sure are strange."

"I'll be right here, mami. I'm meetin' someone out here. They'll be here any minute so you go ahead, sweetie."

He watched her sashay into the hotel and disappear inside carrying her shopping bags. *Damn,* he thought. *She a hot little one!*

A few minutes passed before a burgundy Denali pulled up inside of the parking lot and parked beside Ghostman's Level 5 bomb-proofed/bullet-proofed SUV. He immediately recognized the dark-skinned driver as the big homie, B'More Deuce, from Baltimore Rolling 60's Crips.

Ghostman's truck was backed into the parking space. Deuce's vehicle was facing the opposite way which meant that the two men only had to let their windows down to speak from their respective driver's side seats.

"Ghost," the gangster Crip greeted him.

"Deuce," Ghostman acknowledged. "Cash App that bread, homie."

Deuce opened up a black case and removed an iPad. While he did that, Ghostman used the dashboard computer to log into his own Cash App to wait for the $100K transfer to be completed. Within seconds he confirmed the transaction. Ghostman nodded and handed Deuce a set of car keys.

"The black Hyundai across the street at Wendy's," Ghostman told him.

Deuce handed the keys to the young woman who sat next to him in the front passenger's seat.

"Look here, Dee," Ghostman stated solemnly. "All this move-ment out here on these roads is dangerous. What we doin' more and more of is usin' the Dark Web to do business."

"We don't know how to do all that shit," Deuce complained.

"The monster has gone digital. Why travel up to New York for two bricks of heroin when you can do it from your bedroom in Baltimore? You can purchase bitcoin or make the cash transfer to our offshore accounts in the Caymans. Your package will be overnight delivery or in some cases-same day."

"Who'll deliver it?" Deuce asked.

"Depends," Ghostman shrugged. "Could be FedEx, UPS, U.S. Mail... Depends on who we route it through. Could come from Canada, London, Spain, China, or all of the above. The encryption levels are mind boggling but you'll get it. What I'll do, like I'm doin' for everyone, is sending our tech folks to you to walk you through everything you need to do to begin. Trust us on this. It makes no sense to get arrested at the deal... or on the road comin' from the deal. Plus, all the time you gotta spend travelin', stayin' in hotels... Fuck all that. The prisons are full of cats who ain't wanna change with the times."

"Send 'em on down to train us then," Deuce said, shaking his head. "And I'll train my other peoples. You right, Ghost. We up and down this road, guns in the car, and everything."

"See?" Ghostman said. "You think it's easier to trust us face to face... Man, we tryna stay free! Fuck the money and drugs. We're buildin' the digital world of drugs based on reputation the same as Amazon or Walmart. We guaranteein' our shit just like them, niggas."

Deuce departed soon after that.

Ghostman didn't have to wait long before the pretty teenaged Dominican girl returned to the truck and climbed inside. She placed her bags on the backseat and smiled at him.

He sniffed the air around her. "Look who smells less stinky now."

She burst out laughing. "I did not stink! I'm a girl and a clean girl likes bein' one hundred percent."

He pulled out of the parking lot. "I'm just playin' with you... you smelled like an angel then and you smell like one now."

"Flattery will get you everywhere," she said, loving his compliments. "That purple got me feeling mad mellow. I showered and laid down on that big ass bed up there to dry off for a few minutes. I almost fell asleep."

"So," he said as he drove towards the I-95. "Where you wanna go?"

She thought about it. "It's Friday so... how about you just surprise me?"

"Be careful what you ask for."

CHAPTER THREE

Nyack Police Department HQ
Nyack, NY
Friday, 12:59 PM

Joker had been interested in meeting and retaining Mecca Montecristo for about two months now. She was a rising star, only 30 years old, tall for a woman at 5 feet 10 inches. Her father met and married her Italian mother but their marriage had been short lived when her father had been arrested for corruption in Nigeria before Mecca's birth.

Feeling betrayed by her husband's lies, Mecca's mother had returned to Italy, gave birth to Mecca, and that's how Mecca obtained the surname Montecristo- after her mother, Caterina Montecristo. Mecca had been schooled in the best Montessori institutions in Milan, Italy. When she was 16, Mecca had made up her mind to be an attorney and set her sights on New York University. Her 4.5 G.P.A. had gotten her a full scholarship at NYU where she obtained her law degree within six years.

She had been a highly sought after recruit by several prominent law firms but the one that had won her over was Atwater & Norris. Their offer not only paid off all her college debt but provided her with a partnership after her first year at the firm. She was not just an exotic, dazzling woman to look at but she was a once in a generation, truly talented lawyer that the legal community quickly learned to revere.

Criminal cases were her greatest strength and that governed her a lot of notoriety not just in New York but around the country. *Rolling Stone Magazine* had featured her in an article following her victory in a murder trial where a teen mother had been accused of drowning her newborn baby. In that same article *Rolling Stone* highlighted a growing list of defendants that she had "gotten off" of disgusting charges such as the infamous "Craigslist Rapist" where the rapist had confessed.

"That's laughable," she told **Rolling Stone** *in the article. "The cops violated the defendant's constitutional rights under the sixth amendment when they failed to read him his Miranda Rights. Not only that but the police used a jailhouse snitch to interrogate him which is in clear violation of 'Massiah versus United States.' The court properly excluded the so-called confessions and the state had no DNA of my client at any of the crime scenes."*

Donna Rotunno, the Chicago-based attorney who had defended Harvey Weinstein in his New York rape case, had attempted to hire Mecca. Moving forward on Mr. Weinstein's Los Angeles rape case as well as on his criminal appeals, Mecca had studied the Weinstein files after Ms. Rotunno's firm had paid her an exorbitant consultation fee.

She declined to join the case telling Donna Rotunno, *"I have absolutely no sympathy for the so-called victims in this case because they were driven by wanton greed. Moths are driven to the flame by instinct not intellect. Those women had intellect. They were burned because they chose to be burned. The entire world knew this guy was sleazy but they still chose to get close to the flame. I hate cases like this. I hate the Bill Cosby case because what man is not guilty of trying to get a woman high or drunk so she can loosen her inhibitions? Bill and Richard Prior were doing what they were doing since Uptown Saturday Night! I don't believe for a second that these women are defenseless 'damsels in distress.' Where's the responsibility of women in this country? Women have the right to vote, to be doctors, and fight in the military... all these battles women have won. But when it's convenient, women are weak victims who don't know what's in our drinks or what we may have smoked?"*

"I mean, well I agree," Donna had replied to her. "The media accused me of victim shaming."

"I thank you for considering me," Mecca had told Ms. Rotunno. "But the politics of this case and the blood thirsty appetite of Americans who love to see titans fall makes me decline this case. I don't take cases based on money alone... I take cases I know I can win. There's no winning here."

Nearly all of the cases she took on created controversy from the very start. She was a courtroom brawler, a bulldog, and she loved to win. She made partner with Atwater & Norris (now Atwater, Norris, & Montecristo) and now there was no turning back.

———

Nyack Police Dept. HQ.

Joker saw the lovely caramel-hued attorney and his mind immediately compared her to two music stars: Saweetie, the rap star, and Irene Cara, the pop singer from the iconic *Fame* movie. Irene had this beautiful flowing hair and flawless skin and Saweetie had eyes and lips to die for. Joker shook his head and smiled to himself as he pulled the Caddy into the parking space next to her white Toyota Camry.

"Mecca Montecristo?"

She had gotten out of the car carrying a medium sized attached case. "Mr. Hodges?"

He shut the Cadillac door and surprised her by ignoring her

outstretched hand and hugging her. They both wore black masks to safeguard from covid-19.

"Okay," she patted his shoulder. "It's a pandemic. Don't do that again."

"You know you needed a hug."

"A hundred grand is a lot of money," she told him as they stood between their cars. "Who did your wife kill?"

Joker shook his head. "My wife, Uzenna, her two sisters, one Asian girl, and eight white girls were all victims of sex traffickin' by members of the Brooklyn Mafia. Not even a year ago yet. I met her–"

"Your wife Uzenna..."

He nodded yes. "Uzenna Moses then. I met her after my release from prison for arson and G.T.A. At that release party, my cousin was found murdered the next day in the bathroom stall. I'm a suspect. I started to secretly date Uzenna and learned that she and twelve women were sex slaves to the Mob and I concocted a plan to help free them. Miraculously, the strip club they worked at got attacked with military might."

"You mean The Villa Nightclub?"

"That's it."

"Continue."

He goes on. "I'm the owner of EIE, Inc. We're a band of brothers and sisters... Most of us are former Army and Marine combat/infantry solders. We don't have to hide that. The police suspect us in bank robberies, national drug trafficking, murders, and who knows what else. Anyway, I took in the girls..."

"All thirteen girls?"

He nodded affirmatively.

"Are any of them underage?"

He shook his head. "I helped them get new lives, stolen identities, to help hide them from those animals."

"At least you got a wife out of it right?"

He thought about that. "There's a lot of layers to this. For now...

these gung-ho NYPD detectives who got it out for me are puttin' pressure on Uzenna to testify against me. What they are doin' are jeopardizing the lives of thirteen beautiful girls who I've managed to keep safe until now."

"Will Uzenna talk?"

"Not a chance," Joker replied. "None of them will. I'm tellin' you... these chicks are a different breed, like myself. We're cut from a different cloth."

"Let's go on in," she prompted him.

"I paid you how I paid you because I did my homework on you," he said. "You charge $300 an hour, right?"

She nodded. "That's correct."

"Not anymore you don't," he informed her. "I'm payin' you $500 an hour. I want you to exclusively represent me and my girls if anything comes of this stolen identity bullshit. And, if anything else arises from the police and federal investigations against me for The Villa hit, that bathroom murder, or anything else they wish to manufacture."

They walked into the police station and Joker took a seat in the waiting area near some vending machines. Mecca walked up to the sergeant's desk and demanded to see Uzenna Hodges.

"She is being questioned by NYPD detectives and she has a constitutional right to have counsel present during questioning," Mecca was adamant.

"If you will please give me a minute, Ms.?" The scraggly haired police sergeant spoke calmly.

"Montecristo," she repeated. "Mecca Montecristo of Atwater, Norris, & Montecristo."

The female desk sergeant spoke briefly on the telephone. She nodded her head and pointed at a light blue door and was searched by another female officer before she was buzzed through. On the other side of the door she was met by the black Nyack Police Department Lieutenant, Andrew Hanston.

"Right this way, ma'am," he ushered her down a hallway and

through a door labelled Interview Room 3. To the left side of the room sat Uzenna Hodges and to the right sat the two NYPD detectives.

"Uzenna Hodges, I'm Mecca Montecristo, from the law firm Atwater, Norris, & Montecristo," the powerful attorney stated, shaking her hand. Mecca was struck by how beautiful she was.

"Hi!" Uzenna beamed at her.

"Mecca Montecristo," Detective Pope stated. "It's hardly even a case and you show up here?"

"Detective Pope, Genovese," Mecca acknowledged the two offi-cers. "If that's true, then why are you here? Well out of your own jurisdiction. I wonder... does your captain even know that y'all are in Rockland County today? Maybe I should call him and ask?"

"Well, she was making a voluntary statement," Pope told her.

Mecca glanced at Uzenna. "Statement?"

Uzenna filled her in. "I spoke about my abusive father, my alco-holic mother... runnin' away from rape at home only to be duped into bein' sex trafficked by the Mafia."

"Okay," Mecca sat down. "And now it's over."

"We could easily charge her and her twelve cohorts with a list of stolen identity crimes," Pope told Mecca.

Mecca laughed, her voice dripping with sarcasm, as she warned the detectives, "You sure you want to retaliate against these women for refusing to cooperate against my client? He's married to her!"

"There's twelve others," Pope said.

"Did you know they have some sick sex cult thing goin' on?" Genovese informed the attorney. "You didn't know!"

Pope stood up. "He married Uzenna... She's pregnant now. And all twelve of the other girls are also pregnant."

"It's all consensual," Uzenna explained. "You make it sound perverted when it's anything but. It's love, it's planning, and it's somethin' beautiful. It's not a sex cult. We all love each other and we now have what we never had: A family. All our lives, we have been fucked around. Joker Red gave us back our control, our dignity, and we have undyin' love and loyalty to him, our unborn, and to one another."

Mecca was not bothered at all. "The NYPD need to leave these people alone. If not, we'll take it to the media. These girls have a narrowing, heart-breaking story to tell."

"And now they have another one," Pope added.

"They still be the victims either way," Mecca shrugged nonchalantly. "You want to threaten to arrest, or arrest them, for trying to hide and find their way after escaping sex trafficking?"

"And look at how they were freed," Genovese said. "By their Army vet husband and boyfriend's band of killer mercenaries who assassinated dozens of Mafia members at The Villa Nightclub attack."

Mecca was done with it. "*Alleged* mercenaries. *Alleged* assassinations. There's no evidence of this. My client has a bonafide alibi that you yourselves checked out and the feds double checked it out... Now, if Mrs. Hodges is not being charged with anything, we are leaving."

Pope and Genevese had already been told to not charge any of the girls or Joker for anything less than murder. The investigation would continue. Uzenna stood up and followed her attorney out of the police station. When she saw Joker, she squealed with delight and hugged him.

The kiss they shared was so salacious that Mecca's mouth nearly hit her knees. There was no question nor any doubt the love and attraction between Joker and Uzenna.

"I missed you, Daddy," Uzenna pouted at him. "What took you so long?"

"I'm so sorry, baby," he said as he hugged her tightly, taking in her sweet smell. "I love you so much, with all my heart."

He was rubbing all over her protruding belly, a hand all over her round buttcheeks, and as they were hugging each other, he ground his swollen penis into her pussy.

"Joker!" She blushed. "Are you hard?"

"You two need to get a room," Mecca whispered. "Can we please get out of here?"

"My bad, Mecca," Joker apologized. "This girl does somethin' crazy to me I can't explain."

"My job is done here," Mecca said as they walked outside.

Uzenna took her hand and hugged her. "Thank you so much."

Mecca nodded and smiled.

"My God, Daddy," Uzenna gushed at him. "She is a... she's a goddess! May I kiss you?" She turned to Mecca and asked.

"Hmm?" Mecca shook her head and froze...

Uzenna kissed Mecca's full Sade lips.

"Oh... Okay!" Mecca laughed. "I'm sure you'll call me for a meeting we need to have."

Joker wished her well and she left them in the parking lot.

CHAPTER FOUR

Papa Brneys Sports Bar
Throngs Neck, NY
7:00 PM Friday

Vinnie "The Butcher" Braga had received a text message from Detective Hanna Genovese with instructions to meet her right away. She gave the Mafia Capo the name and address of an Irish sports bar in the Throngs Neck area of the Bronx.

She was sitting in her car across the street from the bar called Papa Brney's Irish Sports Bar, waiting for Vinnie to arrive. She used a Plexiglas clipboard to crush up Oxycodone pills which she then snorted. Once all of the powdery substance was up her nose, she made sure no residue was showing and no evidence off the pills were left.

Within minutes a light tap on the passenger's side window of her silver Intrepid startled her. She nodded at Vinnie and got out of the car.

"I'm thirsty," Vinnie said to her. "Let's go have a whiskey."

Vinnie had eight of his most efficient killers with him as they crossed the street and entered the bar. Feeling the euphoric effects of the powerful opiates, Hanna readily joined them.

Vinnie caught the attention of a waitress. "Hey, doll. I have a hundred bucks if we can get a booth to fit us all in."

"I'll be right back." She quickly walked off to clear a group of women out of a booth they were occupying in the far left rear corner of the crowded establishment.

Once Vinnie, his goons, and Hanna were seated, Vinnie looked at her inquisitively.

"I didn't have to talk my sergeant out of not charging those women," Genovese began rubbing her nose. "The FBI urged us not to because they want all or nothin'."

Vinnie nodded. "What happened up there?"

"I didn't get a chance to speak to Joker Red if that's what you mean." Hanna answered. "I'll return tomorrow, on my day off, without Pope on my ass... She tried to pressure the former Villa girl for detailed of the bombing. All thirteen girls are alive and well. Our friend Joker Red married the one we spoke to and she's pregnant. We learned that not only is she pregnant but all *thirteen* women are pregnant."

"At the same time?" Vinnie wondered aloud.

"By Joker Red," Hanna dropped the bomb.

All nine of the men's mouths were open.

"What's this fuckin' spade − a machine?" Vinnie asked. "He's married to one and-?"

"They're all one big happy family," she added.

"You mean like the Charles Manson family?" Vinnie inquired. "A sex cult?"

Hanna shrugged. "They all work for him at what looks to be a successful store called The Paper Place in Nyack. We visually observed the girls. They're well-dressed, they look normal, and... we only found them because they all recently changed their last names to Hodges and they have arrest records."

"There's been a contract out on this guy's head for months,"

Mick "The Mustache" Dinunzio stated from across the table. "And he's swimmin' in pussy like a king."

"Yeah," said Pete, a big burly man with small fat hands. "Why hasn't he been taken out, boss? Those girls are the rightful property of our dead colleagues."

"Am I really hearin' this right now?" Hanna scolded them, staring bullets through Pete Pouadino.

"Keep it down," Vinnie warned all of them. "We're not here to collect on the contract. Frank wants the guy alive."

"What good is that fuck to us alive?" Mick asked with dismay.

"Shut up!" Vinnie pointed at him. "All yas – stop talkin'. You—," he pointed at Hanna, "...do your fuckin' job! We don't have forever to waste in this piss-smelling city of yours. Here's what you're to tell the spade..."

CHAPTER FIVE

Early the following morning, Ghostman watched as his newest infatuation, the lovely Dominican girl, left her family's house and walked briskly up the street. He observed her cross the roadway and turn a left on Hewitt Avenue, stopping at the Bee-Line bust stop on North Avenue.

He slowly pulled up to the bus stop and rolled the window down on the front passenger side door. All he had to do was smile and her face lit up when she saw him. Without any prompting, Bianca hopped into the front seat of the beautiful new truck he drove.

"Hey, Blue!" She called him by his alias name. "This isn't the Caddy truck!"

He nodded. "You're right. This is my Denali. You like it?"

"I love it," she told him. "I'm surprised to see you! I had so much fun yesterday."

"Yeah, we was chillin'," he agreed.

"But even though I was in by midnight, my dad was still like 'where were you?'," she complained. "He still thinks I'm a little girl."

"Where you headed?" she said. "I'm supposed to babysit."

"What if I hire you for today?" He wanted to know. "How much were you bein' paid?"

"Fifty I think," she guessed.

"Open the bag on the backseat," he told her.

Bianca looked behind her as he drove the Denali into the far end of a Catholic Church parking lot. He parked underneath a large maple tree before turning his attention back to the young beauty.

"Okay..." She murmured as she unzipped the bag, gasping at what she saw. "Oh my God..!"

The bag was filled with rolls of rubber-banded cash. Ghostman removed a hundred dollar bill from the bag and gave it to her. He got out of the luxury SUV and placed the bag into a secure compartment in the back before entering the rear seats.

"Come here, mami," he called to her. "Just climb on back here with me."

She looked furtively around, hesitantly, but she climbed all the way back to where he sat. He used a remote control to turn on some music from Keith Sweat, with "Make It Last Forever" playing first.

"How much you need, mami?" Ghostman asked her in a deep, sexy whisper. "How much you want? I'll give you everything you ever dreamed of. Just be my forever girl."

As he sweet-talked her, he kissed her sweet lips, causing Bianca to melt as he stuck his tongue deeply into her wet mouth while placing several more hundred dollar bills into her hand.

"You taste so good, baby," he breathed as their tongues danced. "Don't be shy... take this cash. You have no idea how rich I am."

Right there in the backseat, Ghostman undressed Bianca while simultaneously undressing himself, assuring her that no one could see or hear them. She was breathtakingly beautiful and her skin looked very similar to the color of Zoe Saldana, the actress from *Colombiana* and *Guardian of the Galaxy*. He kept in mind that she was a virgin. However, he could already smell the aroma of her arousal wafting up from her musky pussy. It was the scent of innocence.

"Show me what you know, mami," he whispered to her as he pushed her downward on the seat.

Bianca licked her lips but quickly sat back up on the seat. "I don't really know how to suck one..."

Ghostman looked at her. "So you..."

"Sorry, I lied," she said.

"That's okay... I'll teach you. Now, get down in front of me and get on your knees," Ghostman commanded and Bianca moved into position. Taking both of her hands, he guided her left hand around his huge ball sack and her right hand around the thick trunk of his pulsating cock. "This is what you call a monster dick, baby. What you're gonna do is give me a nice long blowjob."

She closed her eyes in the rapture as he rubbed his dick all over her face.

"Smell it all over first," he instructed her. "A girl gotta know her man smells good. Smell my balls too. Kiss it all over next." He sounded so sexy and seductive.

Feeling like she was in a trance, Bianca smelled him and moaned blissfully. "You smell so good!" She kissed his big cockhead and couldn't wait to taste him. Putting the tip of his member against her lips, she opened wide, allowing him to ease only about four inches of his mighty length into her mouth.

"That's good, my Spanish Angel," he said. "You can't get it all... Now start suckin' it in and out."

She wrapped her lips even tighter around his rigid tool and bobbed her head back and forth, sucking on his dick and rolling her tongue around the head. "Yeah," he groaned. "Now play with my balls real gently." She kept sucking as she massaged his balls with both saliva-soaked hands. Looking up at him, she smiled around his cock, moaning softly to herself. It was wonderful. She never knew she could be so turned on. Bianca took that stiff dick out of her mouth, licked all the way from the tip to the base, and then down to his balls, putting each of his golf ball-sized balls into her mouth, one at a time, and swirling them with her tongue as she pumped his saliva slick shaft with her hand. "You are one fine cocksucker," he told her.

"I love your big dick," she declared in a sultry voice, looking into his eyes. "I love the salty sweet pre-cum."

"I want you to suck and swallow all the cum ready to explode from my balls," Ghostman groaned as she took him back inside of her mouth. "If you swallow every drop... I'll suck your pussy and swallow every drop of your pussy cream. Okay?"

The dirty way he spoke to her made her moan, prompting a mini-orgasm. Ghostman played with her small tits, and then took her head in both hands and began pumping his dick in and out of her mouth. Bianca held onto his thighs and tried to breathe through her nostrils and relax her throat as he pumped.

"That's it, mamacita," he said. "Take my cock all the way in... suck on it. Don't think... just do." Bianca kept taking him until he pushed his monster dick all the way down her throat, triggering him to groan in ecstasy. Her nose was buried in his pubic hair while his balls were slapping against her chin. She loved the sensation of having his dick all the way in her mouth, causing her lips to swell some.

"Touch your pussy and let me smell the wetness!" Ghostman demanded. "I love the sweet scent of pussy."

She touched herself and whimpered, simultaneously bringing her fingers up to his face. Ghostman clutched her hand against his nose, breathing in her moist arousal. He pumped back and forth, fucking her mouth until he cried out. His dick spewed out a massive load of white-hot semen into her throat, which she barely got to taste because it shot straight down her esophagus. That only got her more excited and she kept sucking and licking the cream from his rod until it was shiny and clean.

"Come here, bonita," he said, pulling her up and kissing her tenderly. "That was your first dick suck, huhn?"

"I love sucking you, papi."

Ghostman licked all over her neck, down to her small breasts, biting her pencil eraser-sized nipples. He laid across the back seat. "Sit your pussy down on my face, baby... Put that ass in my face so I can see and taste everything."

"Are you supposed to do that?" Bianca asked, her shyness completely gone. "A boy once told me that it was disgusting to eat pussy."

"Mamacita," he told her. "Look at how fast my dick is getting' hard again."

"That's because I'm so turned on by you and how sweet your virgin pussy smells. Now sit that tight little asshole right over my nose and your juicy slit right on my mouth so I can drink your delicious cum."

Her pussy was hairy but so soft. Her anus was tiny and puckered like a belly button. He kissed that soft, tiny mouth, then put out his tongue. She groaned when he speared his tongue inside her asshole.

"Oh, that feels good," she sighed. "So damned good!" She cooed.

He circled her sphincter with the tip of his tongue, flicking at it. Bringing his hand up to her crotch to play with her pussy, Ghostman discovered that her own hand was already there, rubbing her clit. She was so wet that he easily slipped a finger between her lips, quickly finding that her hymen was indeed intact.

He couldn't stand it. Before she knew it, Ghostman had flipped Bianca onto her back across the leather seat and buried his face into her wet virgin pussy. Her pussy lips were begging to be sucked. "Hold yourself open, angel. So I can see your clit!"

Bianca used her fingertips to hold her cunt lips apart, showing him the slippery pinkness inside. Sticking out his tongue, he lapped the little button at the top of her slit. She pushed her pussy against his face, wanting more. He sucked hard on her clit, then circled her virgin fuckhole with his tongue, depriving her the orgasmic earthquake she teetered on.

It was time to make his move.

He asked, "do you want me to fuck you?" This was the moment of truth. Now that he had primed her this well, he knew she couldn't refuse him.

She nodded timidly. "Please... Please, fuck me."

Easing between her legs, Ghostman used his pulsating, plum-sized cockhead to push apart her sweet pussy lips. Bianca was afraid that it wouldn't fit, but he coaxed her into relaxing before plunging straight past her thin hymen. She cried out in pain but held onto his muscular back and biceps.

"Open your eyes, mi amor," he encouraged her. "Now it only gets better. Adjust to my size... Kiss me. Kiss the Devil, baby."

Bianca moaned into his mouth and kissed him.

"My little Catholic school hottie. They been teachin' you not to sin, huhn?"

She nodded as she allowed more of his enormous length inside of her moist depths. She spread her legs further apart, whining in pain and pleasure.

"But that little pussy been on fire!" He said as he felt her become wetter. "You been goin' to church... to class... to confession... with pussy juice all in your panties! Haven't you?"

"I dreamed of fuckin' my teacher every day!" She admitted. "Thank you for fucking me!"

"You gonna be my Catholic school slut now?"

"Oh God yes!" She screamed and nibbled his ear. "I'll be your slut, Papi!"

"You want me to be your *personal* Devil?" He started to power fuck her now.

"Hell yeah! Fuck me deeper!"

He held her hands locked above her head and choked her with the other while the weight of his body thrust wildly into her. From out of nowhere, he let her hands go and punched bone-cracking blows down onto her shocked face as the evil who all humanity feared took control of him.

"*I'm* your Devil..." He whispered down at her lifeless body. He knew she was dead but that only served to turn something more maniacal on him.

He lifted her legs and continued to fuck her until he ejaculated inside of her. When he finished, he sat up to catch his breath. The church parking lot had filled up with people who were there to attend Saturday Mass.

He was drenched in sweat. He dressed himself and drove all the way to New Jersey. He stopped at a hardware store where he purchased an ax. He went to another store to purchase heavy duty plastic bags and a rug. Lastly, he stopped at a supermarket where he purchased forty pounds of pork and several gallons of lard.

He found a wooded area out near Saddle River where he had enough cover to butcher Bianca's body with the ax. He ruthlessly chopped her up into small pieces and laid out the rug he'd purchased. He first saturated it with the pork lard and put the forty pounds of pork onto it. Lastly, he placed the chopped up remains of her body onto the rug.

He soaked everything with kerosene and gasoline before rolling the rug up as tightly as he could and binding it up securely with some steel twine. Then he lit it on fire. As he known prior to the plan of getting rid of the body, the flames only engulfed the rug for a short time. The whole point of the pork and the lard was to make the rug burn out, even the teeth would be ash. It was a technique that Ghostman had used over and over to cover up his dark crimes of the past...

To be a serial killer, under the legal definition, one had to kill three or more people. Ghostman's deadly thirst for young female blood was way past three.

CHAPTER SIX

The Indian Sun Condos
Nyack, NY
Saturday, 11:00 PM

Joker had woken up to ravenous hunger just prior to eleven o'clock Saturday evening. He had fallen asleep earlier after a steamy orgy/lovemaking session with Uzenna, White China, Romie, Iani, and Brittani. Walking into the kitchen and opening up the refrigerator, there was a large platter of last night's dinner saved for him. He removed the aluminum foil covering, replaced it with plastic wrap, and put the plate inside of the microwave.

He grabbed a cold bottle of the Dominican beer, Presidente, a fork, some napkins, and within a few minutes, he was sitting down in the living room eating and watching the 11 o'clock evening news on the 86-inch flatscreen smart TV.

By the time Jimmie Fallon came on, Joker had his laptop open, checking all the deposits made into his offshore accounts. He was just starting this daily ritual when the security intercom phone buzzed. He looked at the digital clock on the kitchen counter as he walked past it, wondering what business security wanted at this time of night.

"Hodges," he answered, simultaneously examining the hi-tech security monitors mounted in the foyer. He could see into the parking lot, the rear of the building, into the stairwells, the lobby, and outside of his own front door. There was a clear picture of Detective Hanna Genovese being detained by the armed security at the front gate. "I see her. Let her in."

"Daddy," Uzenna came up to him from behind. "What's she even doin' here?"

"Exactly." He went to throw on a sweatshirt to cover up to his bare chest. Minutes later, Hanna was at the front door with two EIE henchmen who were also an unofficial part of the security at The Indian Sun Condominiums. The whole building was guarded like Fort Knox.

"Joker Red," Hanna nodded as she walked past him.

Uzenna, dressed in an expensive Chanel nightgown, eyed Hanna. "What do you want?" Clearly, Uzenna didn't like her. Joker invited the detective to sit down in the living room.

"With the FBI probe and all..." Hanna was a little uneasy. "Is it secure to talk in here?"

Joker summoned her into the bathroom next to the kitchen. Uzenna followed. Joker had Uzenna search her carefully. She carried no phone, there was no recording devices—anywhere.

"Never trust smart TV's, today's electronics, and so on..." he paused. "This building is secure with its own security as well as a force of my own. To get here by elevator takes a special access key; to get here by stairwell takes a special access key. I own all the condos on the floor. To get up here through my security rings... even the cops would be slaughtered like pigs with the firepower we have out there."

Hanna took a deep breath. "I'm the niece of Frank Braga. I work for him."

Joker Red only took a second to reply. "Mafia Frank Braga? Boss of all Bosses, Chicago Crime Syndicate. That's your uncle?"

"That's right." Hanna pulled out a pack of cigarettes.

"No smoking," Uzenna told her.

Hanna removed several pills from a small container. "My headache medicine."

"Uh huh," Joker said as he sat down on the firm hamper lid. "So..."

Hanna sat down on the countertop near the sink. Uzenna took a seat on the toilet. Joker waited for Hanna to talk.

"Vinnie Braga's in town with a small army of killers," Hanna continued. "They know you don't care about any of that but they sent me to meet with you."

"The Boss of all Bosses died at The Villa," Uzenna said. "So, you're sayin' Frank Braga inherited that position?"

"That's national news, baby," Joker told her. "Hanna's here because The Villa was Mob property that we, that I, *allegedly* destroyed and Big Frank is comin' to collect on the loss. The chickens have come home to roost."

"There has been a hit out on your head for some time now," Hanna informed him. "The FBI had told us about the possibility. I just learned how true it is last night. However... when Frank came to power, he put a temporary freeze on the contract due to the heat put on the syndicate when word got out that Frank was made supreme boss."

Joker Red was becoming increasingly impatient with the pill-head cop. "So, you still haven't said... why are you here?"

"Please," Hanna held up a calming hand. "Vinnie wants to meet with you."

Joker thought that over. *What would EIE stand to gain from such a meeting?* He wondered.

"Could be a trap, babe," Uzenna advised him. "She also said the contract was called off. So what's the point of meeting with the organization responsible for makin' us sell sex for them?"

Hanna nodded understandingly. "About that... some of those sleazebags feel that Joker is in possession of Mafia-owned property."

Uzenna was fuming. "You mean me and my sisters... We're nothin' but escaped slaves to them, huhn?"

Joker could see that Uzenna was about to lose all control and attack Hanna. "Baby, cool it. We gotta play the long game here. Obviously, dude sent his underboss to set the table and it's on our turf."

Uzenna took a deep breath and exited the bathroom, slamming the door open.

"You know Fulton and Willbughby Avenue," he said to her.

"The EIE Pool Hall?" she replied. "Of course."

"We'll have the meeting there," he said. "Eight tomorrow night."

Hanna stood up. "That's all I came for."

Minutes later he was leading her to the front door where two of the EIE henchmen were waiting to let her back downstairs on the elevator.

Joker Red was on full focus. He sent Ghostman a text.

G: Somethin' real big came up. Need u ASAP.

CHAPTER SEVEN

The Indian Sun Condos
Nyack, NY
Sunday Morning

Ghostman entered into Joker's condo and he went straight to the bar to pour himself a double shot of expensive cognac. He flopped down onto the sofa after throwing back the drink.

Joker ran everything down to Ghostman in ten minutes. Ghostman laughed at the end.

"So, this whole time, Genovese is dirty," Ghostman shook his head. "The *niece* of the country's biggest organized crime figure."

He got up to pour himself another drink.

"You know what you call that shit, kid?" Ghost turned back around saying. *"Power."*

Joker agreed. "Big Frank Braga. I'll be damned. At first I couldn't believe it but then it all made sense. He was hopin' a war ain't come... and that's only cuz he put a freeze on the contract."

"How much is the contract worth?"

"That's what I wondered," Joker shrugged. "Uzenna might fulfill it though."

"Why? What she mad at you for?"

Joker sighed, not wanting to speak about it. "Let's get everyone we can down to the pool hall. They have a small army in town I was told so... all elite EIE... none of our young army."

"Full tactical?" Ghostman suggested.

Joker nodded. "I don't think it's a set-up. If they wanted me dead, I'd be at least shot or shot at. No bomb has been detonated and that's their signature assassination tool."

"I can't get over this Genovese bitch," Ghost told him. "Do you see what I see? Braga's in Chi-Town... and he got cops workin' for him way the fuck over here. That means he doin' big things over here."

"The mafia ain't bein' as quiet as we thought they were."

The two men only looked at each other.

———

EIE HQ
Brooklyn, NY
Sunday 8:00 PM

Vinnie Braga was escorted into the EIE HQ office by a son. The Mafia capo only arrived with his driver and bodyguard Pete Palladino. Both men came in and voluntarily relinquished their side arms to show good faith.

"Nice place," Vinnie said as he sat down on the black leather office sofa. To his right sat the dark-haired Pete. Both men wore casual Italian made business suits, Armani shoes, and stylish black trench coats which they removed and hung up on the nearby coatrack.

Joker poured them whiskey and offered them Havana cigars.

They each took a stiff shot and Joker poured them another shot before settling in behind the desk.

"Okay," Vinnie began and paused. "You are responsible for the, uh, East New York thing."

"That's how you wanna start this?" Joker sat back and lit up his cigar. "You sure?"

"We're not the cops," Vinnie reasoned.

"I have a bonafide alibi," Joker said.

"Do we look like we care about alibis?" Vinnie asked him. "I buy alibis and created them every time I fill up the gas tank it seems. So what? That's what wise guys do. It's responsible."

Pete nodded. "It's respectable," he repeated.

"Whats done is done," Vinnie continued. "Don't play us for fools. That's disrespectful. You wanna get far with us... show us some respect."

Joker eyed the two men. "So, what if I did it?"

"*Say* you did it," Vinnie pushed him.

Joker nodded. "I did."

Vinnie exhaled. "Now you owe us. Whatever your reasons were, we don't give a rat's ass. You walked away with our property and destroyed some very important men."

"Property?" Joker contended. "The girls you mean. How are they *your property*? They're humans."

"Drugs, prostitution, gambling, kidnapping, murder... it's all *business* to us," Vinnie threw his hands up. "You were in Afghanistan- how many kills you got?"

Joker shrugged. "Who knows."

"How many junkies have OD'd off your dope?"

Joker was quiet now.

"You just as dirty and corrupt as the worst of us," Vinnie pointed at him accusingly. "So, you can choose a tender moment in Kandahar where you save a small boy... or fall in love with a stripper in Brooklyn. We don't import children and women in from Ukraine and China and chain them to radiators. We target runaways and teenage street whores who are already turned out. We take them in and use 'em for what they're worth. Why, Pete?"

"It's a *business*," Pete finished for him.

"Don't be a self-righteous prick," Vinnie said and downed his drink. "You *stole* our property and attacked our people. We had a quarter million dollar hit out on your head and fifty thousand each on the women you stole. But that was frozen when my brother transitioned to power. Now, he's re-thought everything and has concluded that it would be in our best interest to provide you with an offer of redemption."

"An offer of redemption," Joker repeated.

Vinnie nodded. "That's right. Frank said he would only have a sit-down with you if you admitted to what you did – because it shows respect. You've done that. He wants you to come to Chicago where you will be told the offer of redemption."

"What more do you know about it?" Joker probed.

"That much he wouldn't say," Vinnie answered him. "However, it's an offer you you can't refuse anyway. It means you keep the girls, the contracts end, and once it's all said and done, you'll be more powerful than any other black organization we've ever known. In other words... you're worth more to us alive than dead."

Joker had no choice but to agree. "I'll do it."

The men stood up and shook hands.

Ghostman came into the office after the two Mafioso exited the building.

"What's up, boss?" Ghost inquired.

"We headed to Chicago," Joker informed him.

"Don't fuck wit me, son," Ghost said, observing Joker as he used the computer.

"I'm dead ass," Joker stated. "We leavin' in three days from La Guardia to Chicago Midway Airport via chartered luxury jet. Send out a road team with all our weapons and gear by tomorrow. I'll text them the Air BNB address before they get there. I need to find somethin' nice and secluded outside the hood out there."

"Shouldn't we talk about this, son?" Ghost sounded unsure. "I mean are we walkin' into a fuckin' gauntlet out there?"

"What the fuck is it to talk about?!" Joker snapped angrily. "Since when do we move in fear? If you scared, get a dog or knife, nigga!"

"Fuck you!" Ghostman shouted. "I ain't scared of shit, mufucka! I'm just sayin'... them Italian bastards might be settin' a trap!"

"Who commands EIE?!" Joker shoved the desk forward, roaring in Ghostman's face.

Ghostman stood still. "Man, you trippin'."

"Me!!" Joker yelled at him. "*Not you!! I make the fuckin' calls!!*"

"Calm the fuck down," Ghostman told him. "I never said I wasn't obeyin' orders."

"You still here?" Joker cut his eyes coldly at him.

Ghostman left to carry out the orders.

Joker sat back down, thinking about what Vinnie said again.

An offer of redemption.

CHAPTER EIGHT

The Indian Sun Condos
Nyack, NY
Monday 1:00 PM

Joker used a folding buck-knife to cut open the last of seven cardboard boxes that were delivered form Louis Vuitton Luggage Co. earlier in the day. Brittani, White China, Iani, Ronnie, and Butterfly were all at the condo with him to help unload the brand new designer luggage. Soon after it was distributed amongst them, they were all using them to pack up with.

Ever since Uzenna first learned that Joker was even *considering* doing business with the Italians, she had been particularly quiet around her husband.

"What's the problem, Uz?" He finally asked when he cornered her in the master bathroom of their condominium.

She was busy flossing her teeth. "You doin' business with these pigs who still think of us as their slaves... whores... prostitutes."

"I don't deserve the cold shoulder outta you," he accused her. "If anyone in our house should understand things, I expect it to be you."

She brushed her teeth and rinsed with a cinnamon flavored mouthwash. "I feel like a *nigger slave woman...* owned by a white cracker slave master. They still have power over us and it's eatin' away at me inside. Eatin' away at our baby."

"We *incinerated* those bastards for you because I play *the long game*," he said as he came up behind her and encircled her big belly with both hands. She wore a gold satin Givenchy robe that allowed his hands to glide smoothly across as he lovingly rubbed her stomach. "Them mufuckas are in the depths of hell right now."

"This is never gonna end for us," Uzenna was crying the biggest tears he'd ever seen. "I know what you did and I appreciate it. But they have us all on the internet, on video and DVD's... profitin' off of us engagin' in sex acts... as children and adults."

"And you think once I see them, I'll be ashamed of you," Joker kissed her neck and smelled her sweet scent.

"Won't you?"

"I already promised you that I wouldn't judge you. I *married* you knowin' the truth already, right? I imagine the videos depict y'all in some of the most obscene and vulgar sex acts. I don't give a fuck about none of that now. Y'all are *my* wives. What you want? You want me rampagin' and killin' every mafioso I see?"

Uz took a deep breath and sighed. "No."

"Well, stop fuckin' with me," he demanded. "Because I'll kill *everyfuckinbody* for you! I can't think when you're hurtin'... and it's like you *know* my blood boils where I am so enraged, I lust to murder niggas."

She looked at him through his reflection in the mirror. "No! I don't mean to make you like that."

The veins in his neck and forehead both pulsated with adrenaline. "I'll murder a whole country for you."

She nodded, knowing he was being truthful. "As long as you'll never be ashamed of me. I can't live with that."

"Well, *embrace* that shit, baby." He got on his knees and she turned around. He buried his face against her protruding belly and kissed it all over. "You're my wife now... this is *my* baby... this is *my* sweet pussy..."

"Daddy..." Uzenna sat up on the marble counter and let him bury his face in between her thick thighs. Her pussy was instantly weak with desire. "Ohhhh, God, yes!" He went right where the juice was.

"Stop fuckin' playin' with me." He growled after getting a deep smell of her dripping pussy. Joker lifted her up and carried her out into the bedroom, laying her across the bed. He undressed her and started kissing and sucking her nipples wildly. *"You get wet so quick..."*

The more the baby grew inside her, the more swollen her clitoris and pussy lips became. Her nipples were the portal to her heart and Joker loved how it only seemed to take a soft kiss or pinch to get hard. And he knew that all he had to do to make his young wife's lust go from 0 to 60 in under ten seconds was to pay special attention to her milk filled breasts.

"They're getting ready for the baby to come," he said as he suckled and squeezed each breast. He watched her moan and wiggle her luscious hips until her pussy was locked tight against his right upper quadricep. Pushing both of her full breasts together, Joker went left and right, shamelessly sucking on both nipples. *"I love these pretty titties!"*

Her wet pussy opened up like a flower and gushed like a bubbling hot spring on his hard leg muscle which Uz furiously ground herself upon. Nothing brought her to climax harder than when he bruised his oral lust and fascination out on her sensitive, throbbing breasts. Every time she turned around this beautiful green-eyed man found new ways to encapsulate her soul and unleash her sexual essence. Soon, she was taken to the highest peak they could travel together on in this ride before it all came screaming down.

"Oh-h-h-h, my, uuuhhhgggh, cuuummmiiingg soooo muuuccch-hh!!!" She shouted in the sweetest voice he'd ever heard.

He slobbered and slurped... nibbled and bit each nipple as he humped his muscular quadricep into her squirting pussy. He felt her splashing cream as it geysered out against him and puddled out onto the sheet beneath her gyrating ass.

Joker kissed her lovingly for several minutes afterward and then sat up. Uzenna was curled up in the fetal position for a minute, overcome with the pleasure she felt from the orgasm he'd given her.

"C'mere, Daddy," She begged him. "I need that dick so bad..."

"I'm good, mama," he told her. "Plus, it's too dangerous."

She still felt bad about not servicing him. "It's not that anymore. At least let me swallow your cum."

During her pregnancy she had been experiencing sensitivity and pain in her womb and after speaking to her doctor, a female OB/GYN, she was advised to abstain from penetration. Especially when Uzenna described how large Joker's penis was to the doctor. She had warned that too much penetration could cause a miscarriage so Joker was extremely cautious with her.

"Wait til we fly to Chicago, bae," he assured her. "You can take care of him on the plane. We got a badass luxury jet with a private room inside. Worry about havin' our baby safely. I love our oral sex and all the intimacy we learn about each other."

"Damn, I wanna marry you or somethin'," She declared with a giggle.

"Well, Ms. Hodges," he kissed her again. "I'd marry you all over again, too. Just no more of that shit about you feelin' like a *nigger slave woman* owned by a white cracker... We's a team and this is a long game, high stakes shit we playin."

"Okay!" She wrapped her arms around his neck. "I'm sorry! I was just scared to be judged by you. I know the videos will surface. One of your men will see it and... what man wants to see his wife or wives in sex videos?"

"I murked my own fuckin' cousin!" He whispered harshly into

her face. "In Kandahar, I killed women and children! My boy's legs were blown off in a IED attack one night while we were told not to call in a medic unit..."

Joker had tears in his eyes. She had never seen him like this. He sat up and she rubbed his back. "What happened to him?"

"I gave him his service pistol," Joker shook his head and tears fell down his face as he struggled to speak. "His pain was so great that I had to help him put the gun under his chin and I watched him pull the trigger."

She gasped and started to cry with him. "Y'all were close?"

"All of us were," he said as he wiped his eyes and composed himself. "All the closets in the world can't hide my skeletons, baby. So, who am I to judge you? What you talkin' 'bout ain't shit compared to what I've done. And none of my niggas can judge you either."

"You mean Ghostman."

He stood up. "*Especially* not Ghostman. Why you think we call him Ghostman?"

She shrugged.

"A ghost is a spirit that rises from the dead," Joker said. "That muthafucka was shot in the heart, the lungs, and the head... and still *lives*! He's the most prolific killer to come outta them wars... and he saved my life."

Uzenna's eyes were opened a little wider now about her husband. She'd never seen him break down and cry like that. "There's layers to you that I'm only just getting' to know... but war is war. You can't blame yourself about the women and kids that were killed. And your friend who you helped kill himself - - that was an act of mercy and love. Nothin' more, nothin' less."

He nodded and dressed himself. "Finish packin', baby girl. I got a lot to get done before we leave for Chi-Town."

She got up and obeyed his orders but continued to feel impacted by their previous conversation well into the night.

CHAPTER NINE

En Route to Chicago
Wednesday 9:55 PM

The engines of the C-40 clipper luxury jet screamed as the large VIP passenger plane took off into the night skies over New York's La Guardia Airport. Joker knew that spring was near due to how there were several breaks in the cold wintery weather as of lately. Tonight, it was a cool but comfortable 58 degrees, no cloud cover, and all but perfect out.

Aside from the two pilots inside of the cockpit who flew the airliner, there was a team of five female stewardesses/flight attendants on-board. Joker had brought along as many of his EIE members as he could without leaving the New York operations too thin. As the plane ascended they were all seat-belted in: Joker Red, Uzenna, Ghostman Dinero, Black N9NE, Boo, Knarf, Blaze, Hard Knox, Bonecrusher, Broliks, Fast Eddie Kane, White China, Ashley, Leah, Eden, Louise, Valerie, Melodie, Brittani, Diane, Julia, Iani, Ronnie, and Mecca Montecristo were all along for the trip.

.   .   .

Big Chief, Monk, and Ground War were already in Chicago. They had traveled there a day and a half before with three different vans that were custom-equipped with secret gun stash compartments and tactical gear. Joker did not "feel" any threat but that didn't mean none existed.

"What's the women comin' out here for?" Ghost whispered to Joker. "And the classy new chick... what's her deal?"

Joker turned to him. "I've been trainin' 'em how to shoot sidearms and long guns. You keep thinkin' all bitches are weak, huhn?"

Ghostman looked out at the night sky, ignoring Joker.

"You forgot how they cut open them Italians at the house in Kew Gardens?" Joker reminded him.

"Teachin' shootin' is one thing, son." Ghost said. "Killin' in action is a whole nother monster is all I'm sayin'."

"Who you left in charge in New York?" Joker switched the subject.

Ghostman thought for a second. "A-Son, Divinek, and Meth Man."

Joker sighed. "We gotta get our man Bible outta the V.A. Psychiatric Hospital."

Ghostman laughed but nodded. "He wanna be there!"

"We need more of our comrades we fought with on our team," Joker stated as he stood up. "Help me work on that, please?"

Ghostman sighed. "Okay, bossman. Best idea you had since movin' paper meth into prisons."

"Let me get y'all's attention!" Joker said aloud.

The "Seat Belts On" flicked off of the television screens that were mounted into the backs of the seats and overhead areas around the cabin's interior. Since the large transatlantic airliner they had chartered was a luxury jet, it had all the amenities that the rich and famous were used to.

For example it had thick, beautiful carpeting, Mikasa ebony

walls, comfortable sectional leather seating so travelers could face each other while in-flight. Cassina coffee tables in lieu of the conventional, drab style tables usually seen on chartered flights. There were several 30 and 40-inch flat screen TV's inside of the main cabin, a nice bar in the center, a small bathroom, two large bedrooms with King-sized beds and their own full bathrooms. In total there were four full bathrooms equipped with complete showers and dressing areas. All in all the luxury clipper had the look and feel of an ultra modern penthouse so it wasn't just a flight but *an experience*.

"This is EIE, Incorporated's lead attorney," Joker indicated with a hand gesture towards Mecca. "It is my pleasure to introduce to you the incomparable, the beautiful, controversial kick ass, Ms. Mecca Montecristo."

"Thank you," Mecca stood up and nodded. "Glad to meet all of you."

"You have an accent," Fast Eddie commented.

"And a crazy fly name," Knarf added.

"I'm Black-Italian," she quipped. "I'm from Italy."

"I'm in love already," Fast Eddie took her hand and kissed it. "You can be my lawyer and lose all my cases."

That made Mecca smile. "It's not that much love in the world, sweetie."

"I got some traffic tickets that need fixin', counselor," Ghostman joked with her.

"Oh?" Mecca turned her head towards him. "You don't need legal help, you need driving lessons."

Laughter.

They all laughed and had a good time for the rest of the flight. Ghostman laid down in the small bedroom for privacy. He used a burner phone to scour the various television and online news networks who reported on the missing high schooler Bianca Velazquez. They were looking for her but had no leads. And they would never find her either. He had returned to the clandestine burn site and bagged up the incinerated remains which he'd emptied over the Tappan Zee Bridge into the Hudson River the very next day. If the police checked her emails to him, there weren't any. When they checked her text messages to him, they were to "Blue Johnson" on a now destroyed untraceable burner phone… and he always changed the plates on his vehicles when he was on the prowl so they couldn't be seen on video.

Meanwhile, he meticulously examined SugarDaddy.com, Craigslist, Onlyfans.com, and other Female escort sites for young girls out looking to make money. What he saw excited him to no end. The faces and bodies of some of the most beautiful college and high school girls he'd ever seen. They seemed to be in every state in the country. Posing in their most sensual ways, showing off their cute, innocent, fresh faces and attractive brown, blue, green, and gray eyes.

Chicago, he thought. He researched various "hookup" sites and apps in the Windy City. He ended up clicking on a strip club link and saw a club called Pink Monkey with literally *dozens* of profiles of sexy women. He checked out the photographs of each one. They all had "stripper" names to boost their brand, color, sexuality, and mysteriousness: *Crystal, Tiffany, Amber, Brandy, Cinnamon, Trixie, Lusious, Delight, Capri, etc.*

None of them stood out to him. But when he looked at the girls at the strip club called *Heavenly Bodies* – in Elk Grove Village – his interest was piqued. They had some superstar dancers that looked to be in dynamic shape. When he clicked on their individual videos, he was blown away by one particular female. Out of all the strippers he had ever seen, he had never seen one like her.

She was the club's headliner, it's number one girl. She was tall, 5 feet 11 inches, about 145 pounds, her skin was light, sun kissed, color sort of like peanut butter, piercing slivery-grey eyes, and a full set of pillowy lips. Her breasts were 32 D's and had nipples that poked out like .38 bullets. Ghostman was sucked in to her breathtaking dancing, the hand stands and acrobatic pole tricks. He looked at her name again, Beatrice "Honey B" Samson.

57

"Well," Ghostman said as he shut off the phone. "Honey B... Here I come..."

CHAPTER TEN

The Midwest
Waukegan, IL
Thursday 2:00 AM

They landed at Midway Airport where they were met by Big Chief, Monk, and Ground War who had a nice, chartered bus waiting for them outside of the main terminal.

"A fuckin' Greyhound, son?" Ghost joked when he saw the enormous bus.

"Way betta, home boy," China Man Monk said. "They do tour shit for rappers like Durk, N.B.A. YoungBoy, shit like that. That's what this is: a luxury tour bus."

Inside, they could certainly see why. The bus, though not overly-opulent, was most definitely made for the rich. Joker loved the luxurious feel of having a home on wheels. Plus, once they were on the road, it hardly felt like they were even moving.

"We takin' that same jet back?" Ghostman asked Joker as they sat at one of the curved booths with several other EIE men.

"So, the feds can wire it?" Joker stated as he looked at Ground War. "How the house look?"

"Like a fortress," the big, brown-skinned man replied. "Sixty-one rooms – you'll get lost in it."

"It's bananas, son," Big Chief added.

The mansion was nestled on a high hill area in Waukegan that overlooked Lake Michigan. Because it was 2:00 AM it was too dark to see the majestic splendor provided by the view of the lake but they had seen it on the Air BNB virtual tour via Pinterest.

Although spring 2021 was approaching it was still cold out... Especially in Chi-Town. Fortunately, Uzenna had chosen this particular home because it was temperature controlled at 80 degrees so it felt more like 75 which was comfortable. The owners were a Scandinavian couple who were billionaire software developers. They had several homes between the United States and Europe.

"Fifteen thousand a night," Joker whispered as he and Uzenna settled into their room. "Is this even the master bedroom?"

"Babe," Uzenna smiled as she unpacked, "you see how big this room is? Who cares? And as to the cost... it's a business trip so we write it off. While youse handle your biz with Don Braga, us women will scout Chicago area hotels to see what we can find."

Mecca Montecristo walked into their room. "The door was open so..."

"You comfortable?" Uzenna asked her.

"I think I have the master," Mecca looked around at their room. "You wanna switch?"

Uzenna shook her head. "You keep it. No one is more deservin'. Let us spoil *you*."

Mecca sat down on a red velvet loveseat. "I heard you mention Don Braga..."

Joker helped Uzenna with the unpacking and when he was finished putting everything away, he sat next to Mecca.

"Let's do this," Joker suggested. "We all get a good night sleep, wake up, and then we'll talk."

Mecca nodded in agreement. "Okay. But answer me this. Is it Don Frank Braga?"

"That's right," Joker told her. "Why? Does it scare you?"

Mecca smiled wryly. "I only fear those who hide who they really are. If I was afraid of criminals, I would've never chosen this business, Mr. Hodges. Goodnight you two."

Joker watched her little ass swing as she sashayed out of the room. Uzenna plucked his ear.

"Mr. Hodges," she repeated. "Do you got a thing for that lawyer?"

"You the one that kissed her!" Joker teased.

"Just cuz a woman is cute and I kiss her don't mean I wanna *fuck* her," Uzenna said defensively. "Girls are generally huggy and kissy to other girls anyway. But you all between her ass cheeks."

Joker shrugged. "I'm all between Michelle Obama's ass cheeks and Gayle King's, too. So what?"

"Them old ass bitches?" Uzenna changed into a nightgown. "Then again... this is some sexy older chicks. Who else ass cheeks you be in?"

He got undressed and got into bed beside her. "Serena Williams who you, Iani, and Ronnie got an ass like... Llarisa Abreu from the CBS news in Philly... Diane King Hall from CBS Money Watch... Lizzo..."

Uzenna laughed. "You serious?"

"I'll beat Lizzo's ass – if I was single," he added the last part quickly.

"You better had cleaned it up." She kissed him.

"Who would you do as far as celebrities?"

She smiled shyly. "I wouldn't deal with men. You're the only man I've ever trusted, so... I'd be cool with someone like Cardi B, Mulatto, Saweetie, or Meagan Goode. Cardi has that sweet face and that stripper background so I know she can see eye to eye with me. They all just come off as some sweet bad ass bitches that I can cum wit... don't get me started."

They fell to sleep soon afterwards...

The next morning, they woke up to a giant feast of catered food from a local soul food restaurant in North Chicago not far from Waukegan. Joker had notified Don Braga's brother, Vinnie, that they were in town and settled in at a lakefront home in Waukegan.

Just before 3:00 PM several cars pulled up in the enormous cobblestone driveway of the mansion. Ghostman and Joker observed nine of the Don's goons exiting three fancy black cars: a Cadillac, a Lincoln, and a Mercedes.

Joker opened the doors to the front of the home and all thirteen of his women exited. As instructed by Joker, they cordially greeted the Don, boarding the awaiting luxury tour bus. Joker and all the other EIE men who were in full tactical gear with M-16's and AR-15's draped loosely over their shoulders.

Joker approached the powerful Mafia boss and extended his hand. "Don Braga..."

"You must be the infamous Joker Red," Don Braga said, extending his elbow instead. "Handshaking is a bad habit we must all break with the corona virus and all. Forgive me."

Don Braga and all his men wore protective masks. Joker waved off the apology and bumped elbows with the Don.

"And call me Big Frank," he added in a deep, raspy Italian accented voice. He looked around. "You brought Seal Team Six with you, I see. Machine guns... I hear all of you were in the military. Who's you fight and where?"

Since he was looking at Ground War, it was Ground War that replied. "North Africa, Boko Horam, Afghanistan, ISIS... Tunisia..."

Big Frank looked into each man's eyes for several seconds before turning to Vinnie. "I knew it. I *felt* it."

Vinnie remained silent as they all walked inside of the over-the-top mansion. "What'd ya mean when ya said ya 'felt it?' Felt *what?*" Vinnie whispered as they were led into a spacious first floor living room.

"These guys are the best kind of killer..." the Don said and turned to Joker. "Trained by the best military on the planet. These men are *assassins* with skills we can only dream of. It's in their eyes. That's what I know; that's what I *feel*. They all have killer's eyes."

Everyone sat down on various chairs, sectional sofas, and at the bar. Expensive whisky was poured all around prior to Don Braga getting straight to the point.

"Everyone in this room knows who is responsible for the Brooklyn thing," Don Braga started. "I'm a believer in *what's done is done*. However, there are a lot of my own people lookin' at me... waitin' and expectin' a catastrophic response."

"We *have* to respond," Vinnie added. "If not..."

He shrugged, letting it hang.

"If not," Don Braga finished, "we'll look like cowards and pansies. We live in a savage community of cutthroats. No one wanted to see me at the top... controlling all the rackets. In fact, when word was out that I would be elevated to Boss of All Bosses, there was a plot to assassinate me."

"By other mob bosses," Joker guessed.

"That's correct," Don Braga said. "There have been two attempts on my life so far. One was a car bomb that missed me but killed my mistress and my kid. The other one was a sniper's bullet that struck my vest but broke a rib. I suspect the hit came from out of Philly or New York."

He paused to down his whiskey.

"With that said," Don Braga continued. "We have compiled a hit list of six major crime bosses that you good people are goin' to eliminate for me."

Ghostman laughed sarcastically. "*What?* Six *Mafia* bosses? Why would we do that?"

"Stand down, Ghost," Joker ordered with a cold glare. "Explain."

Don Braga nodded. "You owe us a debt of blood. Yours... or theirs."

Joker knew the Don was not bluffing. Ghostman didn't like the way Big Frank was talking to them and it showed in Ghostman's body language and the scowl on his face. On the other hand, as ruthless as Joker knew himself to be (not to mention EIE members), now was not the time to show aggression or ego.

"We're in Chicago to avoid a war obviously," Joker noted. "So what's behind curtain number two?"

Don Braga pointed at Ghostman. "Maybe your friend here has other plans. You want to shoot me? Shoot us?"

Ghostman was secretly seething. "Don't tempt me."

Don Braga smiled. "You have a gun. They all have guns. *Shoot.* You won't make it outta Chicago. I have three hundred soldiers in this area. And if by some miracle you do get past *them,* you won't get past the rockets that'll hit your plane or the other two hundred soldiers that'll pursue you on the ride back to New York."

"Fuck this," Ghostman stood up and left the room.

Joker waited until he was gone. "Not everyone understands a great business offer. Lay it out, Mr. Braga."

"A million dollars per hit," Don Braga stated plainly with a hand gesture to emphasize what he meant.

That got a rise out of all of the EIE members.

"Cash," Joker pushed for clarity. "Payable when?"

"Upon completion of the best hit," Braga promised. "My word is my honor."

Joker studied the Don's eyes carefully. "That's a lot of money for six men."

Big Frank chuckled. "Your men are elite killers. I respect that. And the bastards I want gone are pushin' me to make *you* gone. Not only that... These same far alcoholic fucks all wanted me dead."

"Want *us* dead," Vinnie added.

Big Frank held a hand up. "We violated many rules of La Cosa Nostra. We've killed other made men without permission, other members wives have been screwed by some of my men..."

"El Chapo," Vinnie reminded him.

"*Fuhgeddaboudit,*" Frank sighed. "We were rollin' in cash for years. First with Roberto Suerez Gomez, King of cocaine out of

Bolivia... Pablo Escobar but his political violence killed him. Amada Carillo Fuentes AKA El Senior de los Cielos or The Lord of the Skies but he died on the operating table... Then finally, El Chapo. We became billionaires *way* before I was boss of all bosses, thanks to my relationship with the Sinaloa Cartel and El Chapo Guzman Loera."

"How's that fit with -?" Ghostman had been listening from the entrance of the living room.

The Mafia Don looked over at Ghostman.

"A billion dollars is a lot of power only if you can manage to wash it," Frank continued. "I made a lot of investments in poor communities with land development, low income housing, built up schools, and sold these properties to the city, state, and federal governments.

Garbage trucks, concrete, construction, fracking, and such have paid us back enormous dividends. Now we have stocks in hundreds of companies here and across the world. But, what made us a risin' star in Chicago made El Chapo *Public Enemy Number One.* That designation put a lot of heat on my soldiers in the streets. DEA, ATF, FBI, USC, HAS..."

"U.S. Marshalls," Vinnie added. "They were the worst."

"They felt we were hidin' Chapo in Chicago," Frank went on explaining. "And we were. He'd want porn stars, strippers, TV stars, and he loved fifteen year old girls as long as they were Black or White."

"And these chicks were brought to him?" Joker asked curiously. "Aware of who he was?"

"Sure," Frank said. "Ten thousand to the minors, sometimes more. I've heard he's paid out a hundred thousand to women he's fucked from Telemundo TV shows. They'd all have to agree to be blind-folded, a black hood over their heads before bein' brought to him, they'd be searched, made to change clothes, no cellphones, no jewelry, nothin' the Feds could place a GPS on. The skies were watched, traffic jams created... all to entertain Chapo. But he gladly paid exorbitantly for it all. Protecting him meant our flow of heroin, fentanyl, cocaine, and crystal meth were protected."

"Meth you say?" Joker leaned forward from where he sat on the sofa.

"Yeeaahhh," Big Frank said slowly, teasingly. "We heard about your little meth empire. Well, I have an even *bigger* one here in the Midwest. That means inside of Chicago and Illinois and all throughout the infamous *Meth Alley*."

It sounded like he was bragging about his being atop the crystal meth supply chain. Because of all the multiple states surrounding Chicago, known as 'Meth Alley,' Joker knew the Midwest empire was a nine-figure one at the very least.

"That's like sayin' you have a dick bigger than mine," Joker shrugged. "What's the point?"

"I *hate* the meth game," Frank admitted. "Always have but I made a deal with Chapo that I had to live up to. Now that he's locked away, I can change the contract... but, here's where it all get's tricky. The Sinaloa Cartel has never stopped it's supply of heroin, fentanyl, meth, and coke to us and I still can't, or won't, say to them stop the meth. I have, however, neglected to treat the meth empire as we do the others. Obviously, my brother delegates all those underworld takes to lower level people. I must warn you that the DEA has been fighting more to shut down meth than anything else it seems."

"I'm aware of that," Joker said. "It's a nasty, nasty drug with an even more extreme addiction than anything."

Big Frank continued in his raspy voice and Italian accent. "You can have my meth routes. The entire empire is yours but it comes with a hefty load of work... or should I say *blood*."

Ghostman was all ears now. This was epic.

"We're listening," Joker assured him.

Big Frank took a deep breath. "There's been rival gangs comin' into Chicago fightin' for territory. The nation is up in a fuss about Chicago's death rate... it's nothin' but street wars. Every now and again, innocent bystanders are killed by casualties of war... it's normal everywhere. Anyway, many cartels, MS-13, and Latin King gangs were in good with El Chapo at one point. But others started flooding Chicago like the Juggalos, Netas, Bloods, and Crips of all types. Now it's really bad and these fuckers are causin' a lot of political heat with the bystander and teenage killings. When Chapo was here there was order... now there's other splinter group cartels here from Colombia, Juarez, Tijuana, Cuba, Dominican Republic, and dozens of gangs running completely amuck. As such we have had our police insiders and our own investigators put together a list of trouble makers in Chicago who have been trying to takeover."

"You mean your competitors," Joker said flatly.

Big Frank shrugged. "Call 'em what you want. There's eighty of them. Many of them are encroaching upon the meth routes. Either way, they are trouble for us all and I propose you eliminate them."

"And what are you paying for the death of eighty men?" Ghostman inquired.

"Zero," Big Frank replied. "Not a penny. The only provision youse get is a sufficient one and that's the entire meth routes we have here throughout the Midwest. That's more than enough payment. A hundred million dollars a year plus. We have all the details, intel, logistics..."

"We have everything digitally mapped out for you," Vinnie stated as a side note. "Including our extensive dark web establishment."

"This is *a lot* y'all are relinquishin'," Joker stood up to think. He walked to the front window with the panoramic view out over the lake Michigan. "Eighty fuckin' men is also a lot."

The shrewd Mafioso boss poured himself another drink and allowed Joker to think.

"Of course we'll show you all the files we have on the six," Vinnie informed him. "And the eighty... the dark web establishment... a complete layout of the land here and all the meth contacts and routes."

That last part got his attention. "Meth contacts."

"I have to be truthful," Frank inhaled and exhaled slowly before answering. "The cartel still supplies these men on the eighty list… so when they're neutralized, it's gonna piss them off."

Joker looked at Ghostman who replied, "So they'll be pissed off. We'll deal with it. I have a question. How many of the eighty are meth dealers?"

"Thirty, give or take," Vinnie answered. "Regarding the cartel, when they approach you, it'll be to kill you so… *you* approach *them*."

"Approach them," Ghost mocked him. "With flowers and candy?"

"We know how to arrange it," Vinnie said. "Aside from wantin' your heads on a spike, they'll also want nothin' more than to sell their products. They'll want a commitment."

"A monthly supply commitment," Big Frank clarified.

"For whatever they lost out of the eighty," Vinnie continued. "That's a lot of dope, coke, fentanyl, and crystal meth. Thing is we don't want to have anything to do with the deal or those particular cartels."

"But I want to remind you…" Big Frank said in a sinister voice. "The only thing you are *permitted* to move in the Chicago/Midwest region is meth. We didn't bring you here to be more competition."

That was already crystal clear. No other organization in the world, other than the U.S. Federal Government, created an 80-person hit list or killed so wantonly. If EIE had any doubts before the meeting of whether the mafia was alive and well, those doubts were now dissipated. Big Frank Braga was the 2021 modern day Al "Scarface" Capone. He was a *ruthless* billionaire businessman and if that wasn't enough power then try adding on the fact of him being the head of the most powerful seat in the world behind the U.S. President: The Italian Mafia in Amerikkka.

"We're principled men," Joker assured the Don.

"I know," Big Frank nodded, reaching over and patting him on the shoulder. "These kids out here today are animals with no respect, no principles, so they need to be put down like animals by the big bad super beasts; principled soldiers with skills and experience unlike anything ever seen in the streets."

Joker was thinking about committing to buying large qualities of narcotics each month from the cartels to avoid war with them. Narcotics that he was not allowed to move in Chicago' narcotic infrastructure that it could expand to its members to include cartel-grade heroin, fentanyl, and cocaine...

"These 'splinter group' cartels," Joker began. "They'll also supply meth and hard to acquire meth-making products?"

Vinnie nodded. "Yeah and you'll need them. There's no way in hell you'd be able to supply the Midwest without them unless you have an army of chemists and key ingredients that the DEA is puttin' a chokehold on."

"I have one chemist," Joker said.

"Use him to train others," Vinnie advised.

Joker had made up his mind. "That six list... we'll have to execute simultaneously so one doesn't tip off the other. All the intel is current and highly detailed?"

"From the very best of sources," Big Frank answered.

"The eighty we do our way," Joker stated. "We don't want a '*D.C. Sniper*' manhunt on our ass so we'll employ a combination of assassination techniques on them."

Joker extended his hand but caught himself and instead the two men bumped elbows.

"So," Big Frank said. "It's agreed?"

"Agreed."

Vinnie handed Joker a brand new laptop and a burner phone saying, "On the phone are the passwords you'll need for the six and the eighty whose files are on the laptop. There's also details about the meth routes and infrastructure here and in the Midwestern region. All info on this thing is highly encrypted so follow the instructions on the burner phone carefully."

"We got it," Joker assured them. "I'm gonna need some other flavors down the line, Frank."

Frank and Vinnie stood up, ready to leave.

"Is that so?" Frank replied.

"I'll need help cleanin' money," Joker told him. "I'm buyin' hotels in trouble, commercial real estate, tryna create legit cash flow, but the illegal money comes in a lot quicker than I can stash it."

"We can fix those problems later," Frank waved him off. "Don't worry. Don't worry."

"I need police connections, DEA, FBI," he added.

"Show me you're *worth* my connections first, son." The Robert Dinero lookalike said. "Handle the six and we'll be in touch. "Remember, you *must* hit all six..."

"Fair is fair." The Bragas and their cohorts left the serene premises.

"Okay, men, lets get to work," he said to the EIE members. Joker turned to Ghostman and said, "We need at least three men in each of those mob hits, homie. The time has come to call in old comrades... I'm goin' to talk to Bible."

"He don't wanna leave the state psych hospital," Ghost reminded him. "You're wastin' time on that fool."

"You leave him to me," Joker chided him and looked at Ground War. "You still in touch with La Colombiana?"

Ground War had a snarl on his big face. "Only when she wants to buy more guns for them drug runners."

"We need her," Joker told him. "Big Chief."

"Yeah, boss," Chief said as he ate dried fruit from a large plastic bag.

"Big Islam," Joker said, knowing how close Chief was to the former Army Ranger turned Mercenary. "Call 'im up. Monk... now's the time to holla at some more of our Chinese and Japanese friends – let 'em know we haven't forgotten about 'em... The same thing with N9NE, Ghostman, Boo, Knarf, Blaze, Knox, Bone, Broliks,

Eddie... everyone we know who fought with us over there, call 'em up! Male and female."

"Clean or not?" N9NE asked cautiously.

"Yeah, boss," Knarf hesitated. "Some of 'em worship the bottle and dope now."

They were all in the kitchen now. Joker opened the refrigerator and pulled out a cold bottle of Presidente Dominican beer, opening it and dranking it.

"Let's see 'em," Joker finally answered. "No one loses what we were trained to do. If we can help clean 'em up... dry 'em out, then we did our part. If so we got killer soldiers on our squad we gonna need for this Midwest takeover."

"If not?" Ghost asked.

Joker shrugged. "If they're so fucked up that they can't come back... then we have mercy and take 'em outta they goddamned misery. We won't turn 'em back out there like lame horses. Can we all agree on that."

Everyone agreed.

"Okay let's do it."

CHAPTER ELEVEN

The Indian Sun Condos
Nyack, NY
Saturday Morning

Once they were back in New York that's where all the plotting and planning started taking shape. The top EIE bosses – Joker and Ghostman – first turned EIE's condo office-study into a war room. It came complete with an enormous 75-inch smart board, six widescreen computers, all mounted on the wall in the rear of the room in rows of threes, above each other.

"Six mob bosses, six computers," Ghostman was explaining. "At any given moment, our six groups of three will be spread out over multiple states and in need of rapid info. This is where they'll access it. Uzenna, Diane, and Leah will receive all communications via encrypted text or phone calls. Their team will reply in the most rapid pace possible after they retrieve the info request."

Two large black leather sofas lined the walls to the left and right as one entered into the office-study. There were a number of folding chairs brought in to accommodate everyone else:

Joker Red, Uzenna, Diane, Leah, Ghostman, N9NE, Boo, Knarf, Blaze, Divine, A-Son, Ground War, Mustafa, Monk, Big Chief, Eddie, Broliks, Bonecrusher, and Hard Knox all were presented for this all-important meeting.

"Y'all already know we've been callin' up old standbys," Ghostman went on. "Most of whom were half a world away like Bushwacker's crazy ass."

"That's my *dog*!" Mustafa smiled a mouthful of gold teeth. "Where'd you find him?"

"Syria," Ghostman replied. "Some affluent family gave him their three daughters to smuggle into the country. He'd married one of them and had a son with her. They made it to Turkey but the girl's mom and dad were killed by ISIS so they all re-entered Damascus to bury their parents. In Aleppo, they came under heavy fire. Bushwacker lost his son, his wife, and one of her sisters."

Uzenna, Diane, and Leah were wiping away tears and they had never even met Bushwacker.

"Where's the third sister?" Uzenna asked tearfully.

"She's comin' in with him on a temporary visa," Ghostman said. "Wipe them tears away, sis. There's much worse happenin' over there."

"You okay, Butterfly?" Leah asked her.

Butterfly nodded. "I'm good."

"The Italian-Amerikkkan Mafia has made a comeback in this country," Joker said as he stood up. "Don't y'all think cuz John Gotti's dead that these fuckin' greaseballs went away. We all probably *hoped* that once the other thing went down. Noooo."

He sat with his back to everyone and typed on the first keyboard until a clear photo popped up.

"Bonanno crime family boss Pat Lombardo," Joker said. "Screen number one."

"Screen number two," he continued typing until another photo appeared. "Colobo crime family boss Vicktor Di Giorgio."

"Screen number three...." he said as he stroked his fingers across the third keyboard. "The great-grandson of the infamous Carlo Gambino, Don Gambino the Third, boss of the most powerful New York crime family, The Gambinos."

"Number four..." he paused as he typed in something else. "The dirt bag Emanuel "Piggy" Santino himself of the Genovese crime family."

"Number five..." he said as he typed and brought up a fifth profile photo. "Big Paul Dellacroce of the Lucchese crime family."

"And last, but not least, number six," Joker said as he pulled up the last profile picture. "Meet Nicolas 'Nicki' Giatorre of the New Orleans crime family."

Butterfly, Leah, and Diane all gasped when they saw the last photo.

Ghostman noticed the look on their faces.

"What?" Ghost asked them.

Joker turned around to investigate.

"He owns high-end gentlemen's clubs in Nola and Mississippi," Butterfly explained. "They literally sponsor teen and pre-teen beauty pageants in the south to target young girls and lure them into this net of debauchery. They *know* if you have a bad home life, if you're bein' physically or sexually abused, doin' poorly in school... they say, *'come to us.'* They have crisis shelters, hotlines – but it's all a ruse."

She had everyone's attention. No one had ever heard her story... there were only whispers. Some EIE members would even tease Joker behind his back for having saved the thirteen women like they were "rescue dogs."

"Of course me and my sisters were raped by our own father," Butterfly continued on. She deeply inhaled and exhaled. "We were bein' recruited and groomed when we ran away and asked for help."

"So..." A-Son spoke up first. "Y'all from Mississippi and when youse ran away from ya pedophile pops, you went to these crisis people for help? And they ended up molesting youse even more?"

"More or less," Uzenna nodded. "It's more details in between but yeah. We ended up with underaged girls dancin' at Nicki Giatorre's clubs. We were on pills and forced into all kinds of sordid-"

"They get it, baby," Joker cut her off. "The files say he owns casino boats all along the Gulf of Mexico."

A-Son gently slapped Uzenna, Leah, and Diane on their shoulders. "If I'm assigned to Nola, I'll send that bastard to hell in y'all's name. I swear it to everything I love."

Joker looked at A-Son and nodded. "Team six... A-Son, Mustafa, and Blaze. Target is Nick Giatorre in Nola."

"We got that muthafucka, Red," Blaze promised. "We doin' this shit for da Butterfly and Baby Red."

"Number five," Joker moved on. "Knox and Bone, I want y'all to get wit La Colombiana and hit Paul Dellacroce of the Lucchese's in Brooklyn."

Knox and Bonecrusher slapped hands in celebration.

"Where's she at?" Bonecrusher inquired.

"That's War's girl." Joker shrugged.

"I like big girls, my nigga," War said. "She just my comrade. Love her to death but she only a hundred twenty pounds maybe... She should be here tonight sometime. Comin' in from Venezuela."

Joker studied the computer screens. "Why's she in Venezuela?"

"She a CIA dark op," War mentioned. "She out there tryna overthrow Maduro."

"Ghost, Knarf, and Chief," Joker said as he looked back at them. "Y'all got number four Emanuel "Piggy" Santino of the Genovese's in Queens."

"I got some new bombs made, too," Knarf said, rubbing his hands together. "I'm *dyin'* to try 'em out."

"War, Eddie, Broliks," Joker called out. "Y'all are team number three: Carlo Gambino the Third in Shaolin."

Not called so far were N9NE, Boo, Divine, and Monk.

"N9NE and Monk," Joker said to them and pointed at the face

on the screen. "Ceasar's comin' in from Somalia. Y'all are on team two. Target Vicktor DiGiorgio in Manhattan."

"Team one?" Ghost asked.

"Boo and Divine... and Bushwacker," Joker finally said. "Target: Patty Lombardo of the Bonanno's, in New Jersey."

"Let's recess for a few hours," Joker ordered the men and three women. "But y'all be back at fifteen hundred hours to memorize all youse can about your targets, the logistics, and everything that can assist you in neutralizing them via synchronization."

Several murmurs of disapproval rippled over the group because synchronizing the hits would be much more difficult.

"What are we?!" Joker snapped. "A bunch of junior high school girls just told their Justin Bieber concert was cancelled? These are six of the most dangerous mobsters on the *planet*. Let's *try* to synchronize the killings so one doesn't tip off the other!"

Joker was about to leave when he turned back around and said, "Oh, I almost forgot to mention there's an even split of six million dollars for this job. *Only* if all six hits are successful."

"By 'even split' you mean...?" Eddie trailed off.

"Meanin' *only* the hitters split that cake," Joker replied.

A roar of approval was heard from everyone in the room.

"That's a lot of money man!" Mustafa stated excitedly. "Three hundred thou each!"

But even as he said it Joker was aware that he would likely change the dynamics because the staked were extremely high. EIE's relationship with Big Frank Braga was riding on these six hits.

"Ay, y'all," Joker said once they'd calmed down. "In Chicago... you was there to watch me negotiate our very existence. And if we pull this shit off, we are gonna be set up to where that six mill ain't even syrup for our muthafuckin' pancakes. Y'all thought I'd keep a lion's share of the six mill... naw, son. Y'all niggas is what got us here."

"Savin' them bitches got us here, son, word," A-Son said but saw the look on Uzenna's face and he frowned. "I'm mean... *Fuck*. My bad. Savin' them beautiful queens got us —"

"Shut up, A-Son," Joker shook his head.

"Shuttin' up." A-Son sat down.

"But he's right," Joker praised what A-Son said. "Boldest shot EIE ever did... Anyways... I'm worried about this one. All elements have to go right or else we are so fuckin' fucked. We stand to inherit Meth Alley, Cartel connections, a billionaire crime boss's money laundering network..."

"Just get the fuck out," Ghost told him. "You blowin' my shit right now. We ain't no amateurs."

Joker grinned. "Fuck you, nigga." He went ahead and hurried out.

CHAPTER TWELVE

The Brooklyn V.A. Hospital
Brooklyn, NY
Saturday Afternoon

Joker was dressed in a magnificent custom-made $3,000 business suit by Armani which was charcoal black with pink micro pinstripes. He wore a crisp pink shirt and a silk tie with blue and pink print. His shoes were black leather, also by Armani; he wore a presidential Rolex, a gift from Uzenna and the sister-wives, and a single $50,000 platinum and diamond wedding ring.

Mecca Montecristo was at his side, also smartly dressed in an expensive pantsuit by DKNY. She carried an attaché case as they entered the V.A. Hospital in Flatbush (Brooklyn) and rode the elevator up to the 8th floor. They checked in at the nurse's station and were asked to wait.

"All fuckin' day," Joker whispered to Mecca as he stood up.

"Patience," Mecca urged.

He waited another ten minutes prior to walking to the nurse's station to inquire. "Sweetie, I don't have all day."

The nurse, a black woman in her mid to late forties, was pleasant to him. "I'm very sorry. But..."

He pulled out a wad of crispy new $100 bills and peeled off one of them for her. "Please. Allow me to do somethin' nice for you and you do somethin' nice for me?"

The woman hesitated. "That's not necessary. Let me walk back here and see if I can —"

"That's what I mean, Ms.?"

"Ellington," she said. "*Mrs.* Hazel Ellington."

Joker peeled off a second $100 bill and pushed them into her hand. "I insist. Now all you need to do is let me and my attorney here walk on into the Psychiatric Care Unit and we'll find our way."

Mrs. Ellington stood up and smiled. "In that case, I am on break and the door is right there. Buzz yourself in."

She walked off and Joker ushered Mecca through the secure set of double doors after pushing the buzzer to the right which unlocked the doors. They made their way to *Room 1202* and Joker looked at the clipboard that hung on a hook to the left of the door.

Inside, a huge dark-skinned man was next to his bed doing push-ups on the white and black linoleum floor. He only wore tight white Fruit of the Loom briefs that seemed to be about to burst due to his sheer size and weight.

"My God, he's so huge!" Mecca gasped.

Eustace "Bible" Reed was 32 years old, 6 feet 5 five inches tall, and 320 pounds of solid muscle. He had been a soldier with the very special gift of prayer and massive knowledge of the word of God. In Afghanistan he had been one of the most prolific snipers the 10th Mountain Division had ever known.

He had earned the nickname *"The Kind Killer"* which no one called him to his face because he would say a prayer for each soul he took. Every shot he made was "In the Name of Jesus." When Joker or any of the EIE comrades would ask him why each kill was made in the Name of Jesus, he would explain that *"These bastards declared jihad against all who follow Christ,"* Bible had said. *"Therefore, on behalf of*

Christ, I humbly accept their declaration of holy war and kill in the name of the Lord Jesus Christ."

"It's war against Amerikkka, stupid," Ghost would argue with him.

"Al Qaeda, ISIL, Boko Haram, Taliban – doesn't matter," Bible had explained. *"they attack in Africa in Europe anywhere and anyone who believes Christ is King. If they can make Christ a lie then that somehow makes what they believe the truth."*

Bible, as everyone now called him, was one of the most loyal men Joker had ever known and he was also a damned good friend. As Joker stood outside of Bible's door, an insanely cute female Indian intern came by.

"We need to get in and visit my brother," Joker said to her.

"Um, let me get the Nurse Supervisor or catch a doctor," the young college student said.

Joker peeled off two hundred dollar bills, causing the Indian girl's eyebrows to raise. She pulled out a set of keys and let them into Bible's room. She accepted the money and followed them in.

"I hope you know what you're doing with Bible here," Tithi Patel warned them. "He can be explosive."

Bible had big droplets of sweat streaming down his face and body. Mecca was in complete awe of his sheer size and raw power. He had a face somewhat like King Kong's and the small beady eyes of a small boy. Mecca had never felt so intimidated. The man looked like a machine and a monster all rolled up into one. His veins seemed to pulsate like water hoses along his arms and neck.

Bible walked up to Joker first and threw his enormous arms around him, picking him up and hugging him for thirty seconds. Bible kissed Joker on the left and right cheek before setting him back down.

"You're my best friend," Bible said and burst into tears.

Mecca was suddenly touched and puzzled all at the same time. She had expected hostility or violence out of this gargantuan of a man but he came off more like Michael Clark Duncan's "John Coffey" character in *The Green Mile*. Obviously, the two men were closer than the high-powered lawyer had realized. Now Joker had tears streaming down his face as well.

"Come on now," Joker chided his old friend. "Let's get it together."

"You get baptized yet?" Bible asked him as they let each other go. "In the second chapter, Book of Acts, Peter said to *repent and be baptized for the remission of sins.*"

"Not yet," Joker admitted. "But, look, I still have time."

Bible turned to Mecca. "Are you a believer in the Lord Jesus Christ?"

Mecca looked at Joker and then back at Bible. "Well... I never... no one's ever..."

"You want me to teach you?" He asked her.

She shrugged and nodded. "Well, um, okay... sure."

"Bible," Joker stopped him. "I need you out of here. I've come to take you home."

"Bible waitin' for Jesus Christ to take him home," Bible responded, referring to himself in third person.

Joker sighed and sat on Bible's bed. "I need your help, Bible."

"Bible stay," he stated stubbornly.

"People tryna kill me," Joker told him.

Bible's eyes furrowed. "War?"

"War," Joker answered.

"Stay with Bible," the enormous man answered.

"Tell you what," Joker said. "If you come stay with me, you can baptize me and tell Mecca here all about the Lord Jesus."

A smile spread across the King Kong face and Bible said, "First I will baptize you in the Name of the Father, and of the Son, and the Holy Spirit... then Bible will crush all enemies."

"Go get the doctor," Mecca said to the intern.

Joker studied the petite young college student as she turned and dialed a number on the wall-mounted telephone. Even in her scrubs he could see the sweet, rounded curves of her buttocks. She had the longest and blackest hair he had ever seen and she looked so good. Her face was oval, her nose small, her teeth even, and her lips were very cute. While Bible spoke to Mecca about her sins, Joker approached the young intern.

"You ever date a black guy?" He asked her.

She shook her head and smiled. "My dad would kill me."

"I'd protect you," he swore, placing his hand over his heart. "What's your name?"

"Tithi." She pointed to her ID badge.

"Take my card," he said, giving her a business card. "I own *The Paper Place* up in Rockland County. I also own some other businesses. You must know I'm really attracted to you and prepared to do whatever to get to know you. I've always dreamed of a beautiful cinnamon-colored girl from India."

She was blushing. "Aww that's so sweet but... my gosh."

"What?" Joker took her small hand in his. "Are you already promised in marriage or somethin'?"

She nodded.

He wanted her even more now. "I know you see Amerikkkan culture and know that ain't fair. You live on a college campus?"

She nodded as he came on stronger and whispered into her ear.

"You sleep at night, hot and wet, about what a man like me can do to you, huhn?" He whispered to her and he watched her eyes flash. "Am I lyin'?"

She grinned. "The doctor's on the way."

"That little pussy's hot right now ain't it?" He whispered to her again.

She let him kiss the inside of her wrist.

"What?" He asked.

"No one's ever said that to me before."

"I know," he told her. "And I bet you dream of bein' fucked real good... of havin' your pussy eaten by a master like me... and even havin' those sexy lips wrapped all around a juicy dick until it cums and cums... How many sex dreams do you have?"

"A lot," she admitted. "Oh my God... I told that to a stranger." She giggled flirtatiously.

He whispered to her, "Give me just *one* chance. What do I need to do? Buy you a car? Put you in your own luxury apartment? Pay off your college loans? Fuck that arrange marriage shit. Let me take care of you."

She stared at him. "Really? You don't know me though."

"There's time for that," he urged her. "Just *try* me is all I'm saying. Just say yes and let me prove the rest."

She hesitated but nodded. "What's your name again? Hodges? David Hodges?"

"Call me Joker Red, baby." He told her. "I won't let you down. And don't fear nothin'. Don't second guess anything. Tell you what. I bet your family in India controls you with their money yes?"

She nodded. "Of course... and with our Hindu religion."

"I'm different. I'll give you your own money. Your own control. To prove this, you go out and find a *beautiful* luxury apartment in Manhattan's Soho district. How does five thousand a month sound?"

She put a finger to her mouth. "It sounds *rich*."

"I got you," he promised her. He pulled out a burner phone and gave it to her. "I know the number to that... I am flyin' out the country for several days and will contact you as soon as I get back. Meanwhile, you start the search. Don't worry about the co-signer, the payment, nothing. As long as I get what I want and need... You can shop to your heart's delight. Includin' the furniture, food, clothes, and whatever else."

Just then an average sized white female doctor walked into the room flanked by two male nurses. Her nametag read P. Dickens.

"Well, hello," Joker stated his most kind greeting to the door.

"Hi!" She said as she walked over to Bible carrying a clipboard.

"Mr. Bible Reed, I see you have visitors today. And who may they be during *non*-visiting hours?"

"My friend and comrade, Joker Red," Bible told his doctor. "And this beautiful woman is my other friend and attorney, Mecca Montecristo. They have come to take me home."

The doctor was surprised. "Mr. Red... You were a fellow solider with him?"

Joker nodded. "Yes, ma'am. I'm the owner of The Paper Place, LLC., in Nyack and New Rochelle, New York. And we're prepared to take in Bible and all that comes with him."

The doctor paused and looked at Mecca, recognizing her from television, *Court TV*, etc. "Actually, Bible is in *voluntary* custody so we can't legally hold him. He's been well-behaved, he's taking Celebrex and Abilify to handle his PTSD and auditory hallucinations... He had initially been brought to us by the police under the *Baker Act*..."

Joker looked at Mecca.

"A temporary psychiatric hold," Mecca said quickly. "Especially if authorities believe he'd harm himself or others."

"You're not going to harm yourself or others right, Bible?" Dr. Dickens asked him.

"The Lord thy God said: *Thou shalt not kill*," Bible answered. "Bible pack up, now?"

Dr. Dickens was a little hesitant. "As long as you return as scheduled for check-ups and that you be sure to take your medicines."

Bible nodded. "Bible do."

"Now, you know about his PTSD and the piece of IED shrapnel inside of his brain?" The doctor said concerned.

Joker nodded. "Ma'am... doctor, I *assure* you no one is more financially and mentally equipped to take on Bible than me. I'm here because I know his own family gave up on him after he sacrificed nearly everything for unit, the Army, God, and country. He has that fuckin' shrapnel in his brain because he saved *me*."

Mecca heard Joker's voice crack with emotion and saw tears come to his eyes. She rubbed his back to show support.

"All due respect, ma'am, but soldiers take care of soldiers," Joker said. "Damned shame. You do all that fightin' and killin' to keep Amerikkkan's safe only to return to have your own family turn on you."

"Pack up, Bible," Dr. Dickens told him. "Looks like your family came to take you home."

"I'll wait outside for you, Bible," Joker said as he walked out with Mecca.

The doctor had Bible wait for some paperwork and prescriptions which he gave to Joker. Twenty minutes later they were all inside of Joker's blue Cadillac truck headed to Nyack.

"You don't mind staying with us at the Indian Sun do you?" Joker asked his lawyer who had already fired up her laptop in the front passenger seat.

"I *love* the Indian Sun," was her reply. "I don't have court but I do have several *Zoom* meetings I must attend. As long as I can have my own space, I'll be fine."

"We'll give you the office-study in Valerie's place," he assured her. "Them girls have massage tables set up, visiting massage therapist, a sauna with music in it, Jacuzzi..."

"Wow," Mecca said as she typed, answering emails.

"That Indian girl back there," Joker started.

"*What* Indian girl?" She shot back. "Hey, man, look... I represent your organization but my *loyalty* is to *you*."

Joker liked Mecca more and more.

"Gotta say though," Mecca smiled that sweet million dollar smile of hers. "It was fun watching how you broke down all of your moral and religious virtues."

Joker laughed at her observation.

He was happy that her loyalties were in order as well.

CHAPTER THIRTEEN

The Indian Sun Condos
Saturday Evening

Joker got Bible settled into the EIE condo where the enormous man was enthusiastically greeted and welcomed by the rest of his comrades that hadn't seen him since they were discharged. To those who did not know Bible thought that he was some crazy "Bible thumper" but men who knew him best knew that he was a warrior like Fast Eddie and Ground War.

"Bible," Ground War cornered the black titan in the kitchen of the EIE condo. "You know what the orders are? You understand why we're here?"

Bible was just finishing up a plate of turkey bacon, eggs, and toast.

"Orders?" Bible repeated.

Ground War nodded. "We're about to go on a mission to kill Mafia bad guys."

Bible stared at Ground War. "Bible ready."

Ground War smiled. "That's my nigga."

"*After* Bible baptizes Joker Red," Bible demanded.

Ground War was puzzled. "What?"

"Ask him. Joker gave word to Bible."

Ground War called Joker on his cellphone.

"*Red here.*"

"*Bible supposed to be baptizin' you, son?*" War inquired.

"*Shit!*" Joker answered. "*I promised. Tell him I'll be over. Shit!*"

Joker hung up the phone.

"You were right," War said to him. "He on his way over. I'll be a —"

Fast Eddie came into the living room carrying a large duffel bag. "We got the biggest shit they had at the Army Surplus… it's all tactical gear, clothes, boots, underwear, socks, belt."

"This big ass nigga don't need no belt," A-Son said on his way into the room. "Hey, Bible… Why you stay in the V.A. so long, son?"

Bible didn't respond. Instead he stripped down to his underwear and tried on the several pairs of black tactical Army pants, shirts, jackets, T-shirts, bullet-proofed vests, gloves, hats, masks, and other items. Whatever didn't fit was tossed to the side and Eddie promised to require in Bible's sizes.

Joker walked through the front door of the EIE condo, followed by his wife Uzenna and his twelve other women. " Come on, Bible. Baptize me."

"Praise God," Bible stated with a smile spreading across his huge grotesque face. He kept on the new black pants and black field boots but no shirt at all. "To the Jacuzzi."

All the girls had heard about Bible but had yet to meet him; they were both fascinated and frightened by him. Most of the other EIE men were relaxing in their rooms, studying the hit files on the six Mafia members they were assigned to assassinate. But when they heard the commotion, they all came to investigate.

"Water's warm, good." Joker took a deep breath as everyone came into the large room. "Great, spectators. Someone get me a towel ready please?"

Eden was standing closest to a towel shelf and gave one to him. "Here ya go, Daddy."

Bible had the gift of quoting verbatim from the Holy Bible. "In the Gospel of Christ Jesus, according to Matthew, chapter twenty-eight, verses eighteen through twenty reads: *And Jesus came and spake unto them, saying,* **All power is given unto me in heaven and in earth. Go ye therefore, and teach all nations, baptizing them in the name of the Father, and of the Son, and of the Holy Ghost.**"

Bible had Joker step into the Jacuzzi, then he continued. "Matthew twenty-eight, verses eighteen through twenty is also known as *The Great Commission* where the triumphant *risen* Lord Jesus sends forth his ambassadors to proclaim the Gospel, *His* Gospel, throughout all the world. These ambassadors of Christ also known as *Disciples,* obeyed The Great Commission when they addressed the multitudes in Jerusalem in the Book of Acts chapter two verses five and six. Apostle Peter addressed the crowds on *The Day of Pentecost...*"

Bible kneeled down and said a silent prayer...

"The Book of Acts chapter two and we're starting with Peter's address at verse fourteen: *but Peter, standing up with the eleven, lifted up his voice and said unto them ye men of Judea, and all that dwell in Jerusalem, be this known unto you, and hearken to my words. For these are not drunken as ye suppose, seeing it is but the third hour of the day. But it is that which was spoken by the Prophet Joel. And it shall come to pass in the last days, saith God, I will pour out my spirit upon all flesh: and your sons and daughters shall prophesy, and your young men shall see visions, and your old men shall dream dreams: and on my servants and on my handmaidens I will pour out in these days of my spirit, and they shall prophesy: And I will show wonders in heaven above, and signs in the earth beneath: blood, and fire, and vapor of smoke: The sun shall be turned into Darkness and the moon into blood, before that great and notable day of the Lord come: And it shall come to pass, that whosoever shall calls on the name of the Lord shall be saved. Ye men of Israel, hear these words; Jesus of Nazareth, a man approved of God among you by miracles and wonders and signs which God did by him in the midst of you, as ye yourselves also know!"* Bible began to speak louder, shouting and crying out the passion of these verses.

Everyone listened intently. Some even had their cell phones out to read from *biblegateway.com* to follow what Bible was quoting. They were amazed that he quoted every word of Acts 2: 14 - 22 word for word. This was truly a gift from heaven.

Uzenna looked at Iani and mouthed the word, "Wow."

Ronnie and others were stood in disbelief as they listen to Bible's amazing sermon.

Bible continued at Acts 2: 23:

"Him being delivered by the determinate counsel and foreknowledge of God, ye have taken, and by wicked hands have crucified and slain: Whom God hath raised up, having loosed the pains of death: because it was not possible that he of death: because it was not possible that he should be holden of it. For David speaketh concerning him, I foresaw the Lord always before my face; for he is on my right hand, that I should not be moved: Therefore did my heart rejoice, and my tongue was glad; moreover also my flesh shall rest in hope: Because thou will not leave my soul in hell, neither wilt thou suffer thine Holy One to see corruption thou hast made known to me the ways of life; thou shalt make me full of joy with thy countenance. Men and brethren, let me freely speak unto you of the patriarch David, that he is both dead and buried, and his sepulcher is with us unto this day. Therefore, being a prophet, and knowing that God had fruit of his loins, according to the flesh, he would raise up Christ to sit on his throne; He seeing this before spake of the resurrection of Christ, that his soul was not left in hell, neither his flesh did see corruption. This Jesus hath God raised up, whereof we are all witnesses. Therefore being by the right hand of God exalted, and having received of the Father the Promise of the Holy Ghost, he hath shed forth this, which ye now see and hear. For David is not ascended into the heavens: but he saith himself, The Lord said unto my Lord, sit thou on my right hand,

until I make thy foes thy footstool. Therefore let all the house of Israel know assuredly, that God, hath made that same Jesus, whom ye have crucified, both Lord and Christ. Now when they heard this, they were pricked in their heart, and said unto Peter and to the rest of the apostles, men and brethren, what shall we do?"

Bible got up from his knees at that point and walked over to the Jacuzzi. He removed his boots and pants and used the steps to get inside of the warm bubbling water.

"They heard the word of God and it cut deep inside of their hearts at what they'd did," Bible explained to everyone. "They had put an innocent man, our Jesus, to death and did *nothin'*! So... what shall *we* do? They asked in Acts two verse thirty-seven. Apostle Peter, in obedience to Matthew twenty-eight, verses eighteen through twenty said to them in Acts two verse thirty-eight... *Then Peter said unto them, repent and be baptized every one of you in the name of Jesus Christ for the remission of sins, and ye shall receive the gift of the Holy Ghost... David 'Joker Red' Hodges, I baptize thee in the name of the Father... and of the Son... and of the Holy Spirit..."*

Bible took hold of Joker Red and dunked him completely underneath the water. Joker squeezed his nose as he went head backward for a second and then upward out of the water. Joker was met by Uzenna and Julia as he exited the Jacuzzi.

"Praise God," Bible went on. "Peter also said in Acts two verses thirty-nine through forty-one... *For the promise is unto you and to your children, and to all that are afar off, even as many as the Lord our God shall call. And with many other words did he testify and exhort, saying, save yourselves from this untoward generation. Then they that gladly received his word were baptized: and the same day there were baptized: and the same day there were added unto them about three thousand souls."*

Julia was first after Joker to get baptized.

"Praise the Lord, Sister!" Bible clapped his hands. "Don't worry about clothes getting' wet! Line up! Come on. Y'all are linin' up to get the corona vaccine... get this *spiritual* vaccine!"

"Do you believe that Jesus Christ is your 'Lord and Savior?"

Bible asked Julia who nodded. "Then I baptize you in the name of the Father... and the Son... and of the Holy Spirit!"

And one by one, to Joker's disbelief, *everyone* in the crew abandoned their pride and went down in the name of Jesus Christ. During the baptisms, Meth Man Ace arrived with the long-awaited reinforcements.

CHAPTER FOURTEEN

The Indian Sun Condos
Saturday Evening

"These is *ya* folks," Meth Man said to Joker as they all walked in. Meth Man had served in the military but not alongside any of the EIE, particularly not in armed conflict as most of them had. "I knew you expected them so..."

Joker was first to embrace the new men and women as they walked into the EIE condo. First was an icy blue eyed white man named Breach, a former marine sniper. Then a tall, leggy, blond bombshell with aqua green eyes named Casci Caliendo AKA "La Colombiana."

She came right in, wrapped her arms around Joker's neck, and kissed him wetly on the lips.

"Casci," Joker greeted her.

Next came Bushwacker, brown skinned with thick dreadlocks. Behind him came a really classy-looking Spanish woman with long black hair. She looked like a school teacher but was a former Air

Force pilot whose nickname was Rogue. Joker had become familiar with her and her other members of her squadron of fighter pilots after several missions they had flown over in Afghanistan.

"Rogue!" Joker scooped the Puerto Rican woman up in his arms. She kissed his cheek. "Hey, Red."

Then walked in a bald, black man most of EIE knew as Pooch. "Hey everybody!" He greeted the men and women of EIE.

Last to walk in was a 6 feet 4 inch hulk of a light skinned man known as Goliath, an Army Ranger sniper.

"How many of y'all is it?" Joker wondered, looking out the door before he closed it. "Y'all get comfortable. I have to go get dry and get dressed."

———

Indian Sun Condos

Joker called Tithi Patel at the Brooklyn V.A. Hospital and she was very quick to answer the cell phone he had given her. She was very happy to hear from him as he was her.

"I was thinking you weren't real," she admitted. *"And I'm still in so much doubt."*

Joker had Uzenna take several naked photos of him before he got fully dressed, and he texted them to Tithi as he put the "shhh" to his lips so that Uzenna stayed quiet.

"Look at the photos I sent you," Joker said to her.

There was a few moments of silence.

"Little virgin girl from India I met at the V.A.," he whispered to his wife. "College intern... you interested in turning her out?"

Uzenna blushed but smiled. "Have her send photos."

Joker relayed that request to Tithi who was still flushed at seeing him naked. Moments later, several selfies of her came through the cell phone. Uzenna studied the pictures and whispered to Joker, "My goodness, she's a *dollbaby*!"

"So, it's a go?" He asked her.

She gave him permission. "Reel her in. She's beautiful."

"I called just to check in, sweetie," Joker told her. *"I'll call back soon."*

"She's exotic, Daddy," Uzenna told him.

"She's gonna haveta wait, baby," he said as he put his cell phone in his back tactical pants pocket.

"Babe," Uzenna stopped him on his way out.

"That girl kissing you like that over there... What was that about?"

"Casci Caliendo." Joker laughed. "You mean have we fucked?"

"Well? She kissed you like y'all did."

Joker shook his head. "We almost had a brief thing over in the desert... But no. Rogue is an Air Force pilot I never fucked but I knew she was down to smuggle guns and drugs. She flies F-35's and shit like that."

"So, she's a fighter pilot," Uzenna stated.

"A damned good one," Joker nodded.

He kissed her. "I need a taste and smell of that pussy and ass later on so... don't go to sleep."

He left her with a smile on her face as he returned to the EIE condominium.

The Indian Sun Condos
Saturday Evening

"Rogue, Goliath, Breach, Pooch, Caesar, Bible, Bush, Colombiana," Joker called from the living room of the EIE house. "Come to the back!"

They all came to the master bedroom where he was sitting on

one of the large brown leather sofas. All of the EIE were also with them when they came in.

"Okay, look," Joker said as he sat back and looked at the newcomers. "They been fillin' y'all in?"

They all nodded.

"Bushwacker's assigned to Team one," Joker told him. "That's Boo and Divine. Stand together... Okay. Caesar's on Team Two stand by 'em. Everyone stand in groups so I can see you..."

They did as he asked.

Joker continued. 'It's War, Eddie, Broliks, and Bible on Team Three now... Chief, Knarf, Ghost, and Rogue on Team Four... Knox, Bone, Colombiana, and Breach on Team Five... And A-Son, Mustafa, Blaze, Pooch, and Goliath on Team Six."

"That 300 bandz just got smaller," A-Son said so everyone could hear.

"So you'd think," Joker retorted.

"Three hundred bandz?" Breach interjected. "What fuckin' three hundred bandz?"

"The job we're doing is payin' six million," Ghost revealed. "Joker promised it to all the hitters... *Eighteen* hitters... But now there's *twenty-three*."

"Actually boss," N9NE started out. "We can handle the hits as is. We don't need five more mouths to feed."

"Let me stop you cry baby niggas right there," Joker held up a hand. "Everyone in this room gets three hundred bandz across the board *if all the hits are successful.*"

"That means none of y'all pussies can fuck up," Ghost said. "One of us misses..."

"They don't pay," Red stated. "Simple as that. So don't fuckin' blow it."

"The mob is paying out six million for the six hits?" Ghost said to Joker Red.

"That's right."

Ghost stared at him.

"What don't you underfuckinstand?" Red stated impatiently.

"You guaranteeing three hundred k for twenty-three hitters..."

"Look y'all," Jokers stood up. "I'm guaranteein' the rest outta *my own* pocket cuz this shit too important not to pay top dollar for."

An hour later Joker was gone. Breach, Bushwacker, Caesar, Bible, Rogue, Colombiana, Pooch, Goliath, and all the other EIE soldiers stayed to prepare each of their teams for the launch off of the hits. The white assassin with the icy blue eyes was speaking as he inspected his sniper rifles.

"There was a fortune out on the table here," Breach was saying. "How much were we paid by quarter to go after ISIL leadership in Syria?"

Colombiana, Pooch, Goliath, Rouge, Caesar, Breach, and Bushwhacker were all on the payroll of mercenary group *Blackwater* and they were also contracted by U.S. Department of Defense, CIA, and other governments, at times, to carry out armed services.

"Not three hundred k that's for sure," Casci "Colombiana" Caliendo said as she double-checked her own weapons. "We don't get paid that much to help overthrow foreign governments."

"I thought mercenary work pays big," Ghost commented.

"Depends on who the boss is," Colombiana said. "The government... Like the U.S. for instance. They want Maduro dead but no direct involvement. So, who do they call? People like us who they don't like... until it's necessary."

"We fly out to Death Valley, California to train at 0400 hours," Ghost changed the subject. "Let's be packed and ready to roll out with no delays. Our flight leaves at 0600 hours."

Ghostman started to exit the room then another thought made him pause. "The point here is clear: Joker's so worried and concerned about not making any mistakes on these six hits that he's paying an extra *mill point five* to the five not counted in the original eighteen. His rep and EIE's rep are on the line here... Not to mention a war with the entire Amerikkkan Mafioso. Any misses will be catastrophic. Any mistakes – *disastrous*. Y'all were not called in just for this hit... But a possible deadly war with the Mob if we fuck this up."

With that, he went to his room to crash for the evening. Everyone else soon followed suit.

CHAPTER FIFTEEN

Tribeca Loft
Manhattan, NY
Afternoon & Evening

After his men and women soldiers had made their flight, Joker linked up with a sophisticated luxury apartment broker in Manhattan named Elliana Carreche from Canfield Realty Co. She met him at her second floor office in Tribeca on Houston Street.

"Mr. Red?" The slender white woman greeted him at the front door of the office at the stairs. The amazingly beautiful Tithi Patel was with her.

"You beat me here!" Joker said, surprised. He hugged her and kissed her. She was shy at first but she quickly melted and allowed him to take her sweet mouth. They both loved how clean and fresh the other tasted. "Wow."

"Come on," she whispered. "You're making me blush."

"That's okay!" Elliana said in her thick Sicilian accent. "I see that you both *adore* each other."

They looked at one another and smiled.

"Well," Elliana said as they began to walk to the east on Hudson Street. "There is a brand new building we have listed right up the street from the offices here..."

The building was literally two blocks up and when he saw it, he instantly knew there was nothing inside of it even close to $5,000 per month because it was clearly designed for people with high-end tastes. It was a luxury Tribeca loft building probably created for corporate CEO's and executive bankers. Joker had a feeling that Elliana figured out that he was trying to impress this young girl who was studying to be a doctor. He had clearly told the broker that he was looking to pay "about" $5,000 a month for something "really nice for my Indian Princess/girlfriend."

"When you emailed me about your Indian Princess..." Elliana trailed off as they were let in by building security. "I just *had to* show you this place. It's a modern marvel..."

They took the elevator to the twenty-fifth floor penthouse loft. The pricetag was $3.5 million and almost instantly Tithi began to protest that it was way too much for her and how she couldn't accept it. Joker took her by her hand and stood next to a triple set of grand arching windows that displayed many panoramic views of New York City's landmark buildings below.

"Look at me," he told her as Elliana stepped away to give them privacy. "Do you feel this?"

He placed her small hand underneath his shirt to feel his chest.

"Yes..." Tithi slowly nodded. "It's your heart beating. Very quickly."

"It's *pounding* not beating." He kissed her full pouty lips. "You believe in love at first sight?"

"Oh my God, yes." She nodded. "You scare me so much... This is so crazy."

They kissed like newlyweds.

"I want and need you so bad," he said with an urgency he never felt before. "You want and need me too?"

She nodded. "I do."

"Let's hurry up and let her show us these places," he told her. "Elli!"

"I'm here." She came back into the large living area.

"Three point five mill is not comfortable for her," he mentioned. "But show us the rest and then we'll move on. I mean I love it and can certainly afford it... but it's too much for her."

An hour later they ended up on the tenth floor in a much more modest loft apartment that Tithi fell in love with. However, it was nearly $12,00 per month.

"Way too high," she shook her head. "You said five grand."

"This comes as an option to buy?" he asked the real estate broker.

Elliana said, "It sure does."

Joker thought it over. "We'll do it as a company purchase. This way I can write off some of it as a business/corporate expense. Place her name on the lease for two years... when you obtain your medical doctorate, you can buy it from TPP. For now we'll cover it."

They went back to Canfield Realty, Co. offices to cover the sales and financial paperwork. The total pricetag for the loft was $280,000. Tithi could not believe it. By 3:30 PM the sale was done and they both were sitting in the waiting area of the nearby European-Asian Sensibility Furniture store soon thereafter.

"This stuff is so *expensive*," She told him as they drank fruit smoothies. "It's all high-end."

Joker smiled at her. "Is your family millionaires, sweetie?"

Tithi thought about it. "I'm not really sure... We're from the north in Bikaner, close to the Great Indian Desert. My father and grandfather own land and livestock... So, I do not know. Perhaps."

"I want to hear all about you and your family and the man you were goin' to marry," Joker told her. "For now... remember that this is Amerikkka and the word is not 'less' but 'more' over here. I am a man with millions of dollars to my name and I made it from zero. From *nothin'*... I had to tough my way through bad neighborhoods and the streets to make it. And here you say your peoples ain't *millionaires?* But here you are in Amerikkka going to school to be a doctor? I thought you had to marry a Hindu husband to keep your royal blood in the family or something."

"I'm confused," she said, pausing.

"No, no…" he shook his head. "That's *awesome*! I felt like your family would put out a hit on me with a bunch of Hindu tribesmen or somethin'."

She smiled prettily, showing off her dark pink gum line.

"Do you feel like you *'have to be'* married to me?" He asked her. "To be with me?"

She was hesitant to answer.

"You don't," he told her. "This is Amerikkka. You don't have to do shit you don't want to do here. However, I want you all to myself. I want to love you, make love to you, and spoil you like crazy. I want you to be my girl."

She got up from where she was seated and sat in his lap. They kissed like teenagers at a movie theater away from their parents for the first time.

"Teach me how to be yours," she told him. "I'll do anything to be perfect for you. I feel so much the same way for you. I will be your girl. I *am* your girl."

They met with a raven-haired middle-aged woman with an eastern European accent. She introduced herself as Susanna Knightengale and within minutes, she had the young Indian Princess picking and choosing whatever she wanted from out of the enormous furniture store.

"I won't be available as much as Miss Patel here." Joker told Susanna. "So please give her unfiltered access to my Centurion Black Card account to decorate the apartment. And we also want to hire you to personally see to it that the entire place is decorated top to bottom. Spare no expense."

"No problem," Susanna established the American Express Centurion account and Joker signed everything. "You work and go to school in Brooklyn, Miss Patel?"

"Tithi," she pronounced it as "Tee-Tee" for the saleswoman. "I actually go to school at NYU Med in Manhattan but work at the V.A. Hospital in Brooklyn."

By 7:45 PM that evening there was a truck and a van being unloaded with boxes of furniture and decorative items from the European-Asian Sensibility Furniture store and carted into the building. There were six male workers that were in charge of all the moving.

Joker tipped all the men with $250 and he made sure they all had pizza and sodas delivered by *Uber Eats*. By 9 PM Susanna was there with the crew of her own decorators.

Joker took Tithi out to his luxury blue 5 level bullet/bomb-proof Cadillac truck and drove her to her dorm building at the NYU Medical School entrance in Manhattan.

"C'mere for a little while, dollbaby," he told her as he climbed into the back seat, in the last row of the SUV. There was a huge 40 inch flat screen TV playing the movie *Body of Evidence* with Madonna on screen being fucked in the ass.

Tithi shyly joined him in the backseat and they locked all the doors. He immediately began kissing her and devouring her mouth with his tongue and lips. He removed her blouse and bra, putting her beautiful firm breasts on full display. He made lavish love to her hardened nipples, causing them to become moist and to throb with joy in his mouth and hands.

"Your pussy is crazy wet isn't it?" He breathed.

Tithi moaned, her clit pulsating in her silk panties. "Um hmm," she nodded.

"Take off your panties," Joker commanded her. "Lemme see what your hot cunt and ass smells like when you're in heat and ain't showered all day."

She hesitated. "We won't get in trouble?"

He ignored her. "Don't be afraid... Do what I say. Take 'em off and stick 'em in my face. Let me smell the *wonderful* aroma of that hot juicy virgin Indian pussy."

"You like it that I'm a virgin?" She asked him. "Or that I'm from India?"

Tithi removed the panties from over her high heeled shoes.

"Both," Joker said. She placed the white silky panties in his face and he got drunk off the musky aroma of her wild perfume-less scent. "Oh my fuckin' God... You use no perfume or nothin'?"

"A plain soap," she revealed. "You don't approve?"

He pulled her down onto her back and took off her dress. "Approve? Let me show you how much I approve. Have you ever had anyone lick your pussy?"

Her chest heaved as she was shivering. "No but..."

"But?"

She was bashful. "But I watch *Pornhub.com* and dream about it while... *you know*..."

"No," he stated. "I *don't* know. Now, you want me to teach you... so, you have to not be shy. Just say what you think."

"Well..." She said, squirming. "I fantasize a lot while... Touching myself."

She had a hairy pussy. Clear juices leaked out of her dark pulpy labia lips and her pink clit protruded out of the skin on top like a wet jelly bean.

"Touch yourself now," he slowly urged her. "Rub your fingers all in it... Get them nice and wet."

She did as she commanded her to. "Like this?"

"That's right," he said. "Now... Stop. Take those two fingers and rub them under my nose."

Tithi did as he asked and he inhaled her warm heady scent. Joker undressed himself and directed her to look at his enormous length. "Look and feel how hard and big it grows. You know why?"

She shrugged as she propped herself up and grabbed ahold of his pulsating, veiny, brown member. "Because of me? My creaminess?"

Joker nodded and smiled. "Yeeeaaahhh, beautiful Indian

Princess. How perfect you are and how lovely your pussy smells. May I please have a taste of your honey?"

She nodded and her lovely pussy squeezed out a droplet of her heavenly nectar. He smelled it as if it was warm apple pie first. He loved her sweet musky scent. The smell of a hot, horny pussy did something to him.

Joker buried his tongue inside of her creamy center first and swirled his tongue around her pussy hole. From there he placed gentle baby kisses up and down the thin seam of her vagina. He made his way back down to her entrance because he loved the nonstop flow of sweet juices that dribbled out of her and he wanted even more of her...

Pushing her legs back, her cinnamon brown ass crack spread opened like a hot buttered biscuit and her hairless asshole appeared. Her pussy cream had leaked downward over her dark crinkly rosebud and his tongue was inside of her within an instant.

Joker went back to sucking and speed-tonguing her excited clitoris. Both of his hands were on her breasts, tweaking her stiff nipples. She melted and had multiple orgasms in his mouth.

"*Ohhh! Ummmm! So good!*" Tithi moaned and whimpered as her hips twisted to and from in his hands. "*You make me cummm so much!*"

"*I love this juicy virgin pussy!*" He murmured as he climbed up her body and kissed her mouth, "You think you ready to take this long thick pipe deep inside of you yet?"

He reached down and fit the large plum sized head of his member flush against her opening. He tried to ease himself inside of her but it was too uncomfortable so he stopped trying.

"I won't hurt you, love," he soothed her.

Joker sat up against the comfortable seating and she kissed her way downward. Tithi got down on the floor and began to make love to him with her mouth. But he stopped her.

"It was *your* pleasure tonight," he assured her. "Ooo, shit, you need to stop."

"But I wanna please you," she begged him, wanting to taste his cum juice.

"You'll do it next time," he promised her. "You orgasmed tonight?"

"Several times," she purred and cuddled against him.

They got dressed and he walked her up to her dorm room.

"I have no panties on," she whispered.

He hugged her at the doorway to the main entrance, running his hands up the back of her dress.

"Goodnight, my sweet Princess. I'm keepin' your panties."

He kissed her and she disappeared inside. As he watched her go Joker wondered how he'd introduce Tithi to Uzenna... and then the others. She was, after all, a Hindu believer... with religious inhibitions. And not only was he a married man but one with *thirteen* pregnant women and Uzenna was almost ready to give birth.

And then he thought about his EIE team...

CHAPTER SIXTEEN

The Indian Sun Condos
Nyack, NY
Wednesday 6:00 PM

"We really need to consider buyin' and ownin' some land to train on," Ghostman suggested to Joker the very same evening they had returned from Death Valley. "It's hot as balls out there but it has that Middle Eastern feel. No better way to train than in the extremes."

Joker had already considered it. "I seen a hundred-fifty acre ranch in Colorado... And it's extreme cold there but beautiful summers. And I'm sure we can find something in Nevada, Arizona, or Cali to fit our desert needs. I'm looking into it."

They were all meeting inside of Joker's condo, having a King's feast for dinner. As the teams were making last minute preparations to launch off, Knarf had brought with him the new C-4 bombs he'd created.

. . .

"Don't worry," Knarf assured Julia and Ashley when they saw the bombs.

"They're controlled by a detonator... Or, alternatively, a cell phone signal."

"Uh uh, Knarf," Ashley stated vehemently. "What if someone accidentally calls the fuckin' number on one of the bombs?"

Knarf laughed it off. "One in three-hundredths of a millionth chance..."

"Exactly," she said. "There's a *chance*. Get 'em out of here. That's insane. There's thirteen women carrying thirteen babies in here."

"I'm just fuckin' with you, Ash," Knarf laughed. "The batteries are not in 'em yet."

"You are such an asshole!" Ashley playfully threw a crumpled up napkin at him from where she sat across the table.

"Anyway," Knarf said, holding up one of the bombs. "Everyone here was shown how to arm, attach, and detonate these suckas. Each crew will travel with two of them and double the attachments to make two hundred percent sure they get their target. Put it under a car, under a bed, wherever he goes to sleep."

"That's only if we can't snipe 'im off," Ghost said, looking across the dining room threshold into the living area near the fireplace at Bible who was kneeling down on both knees. "Bible been praying all day."

Joker nodded. "That's part of what he's called here to do. To help protect all of us murders, heathens, and whoremongers from destruction."

"Who are you callin' a whore?" La Colombiana said, rolling her neck. "I'm a virgin."

Laughter all around.

Bible approached the circle of killers, soldiers, and mercenaries. "Bible ready."

Ghost looked up at him. "What's that Holy Book say about this enemy we about to face?"

Bible shrugged. "Let's see when we open it up."

He turned to a random page and read from where his eyes fell: "And we're at Proverbs chapter sixteen, verse seven where God says: *When a man's ways please the Lord, he may give even his enemies to be at peace with him.*"

Everyone looked at each other in awe.

"It says that?" A-Son came over to where Bible stood. "Move your big ass monster arm out the way, B."

Bible showed him the verse Proverbs 16: 7, pointed to it and it said exactly that.

"Wow," Rogue said. "Praise God."

"Amen," Ghost muttered. "Youse a scary nigga for real, Bible."

"Time to pray for protection." Bible urged everyone to hold hands. And then he prayed:

I will praise thee, O Lord, with my whole heart; I will show forth all thy marvelous works. I will be glad and rejoice in thee: I will sing praise to thy name, O thou Most High. When mine enemies are turned back, they shall fall and perish at thy presence. For thou hast maintained my right and my cause; thou safest in the thorne judgment right. Thou hast rebuked the nations, thou hast destroyed the wicked, thou hast put out there name. For ever and ever. Amen.

Psalm 9:1 – 5.

Everyone repeated "Amen."

"Bible ready to roll."

Ghost lit up. "We rollin'!"

———

The Tribeca Loft
New York, NY
Thursday Afternoon

To keep from going crazy with worry over the impending mob boss hits, Joker spent the previous night making love with all of his women. He had taken Viagra to stay supercharged and although they were pregnant, they seemed to be on hyper sex mode themselves. He let each of them ride on top of him since the control gave them more power over their own orgasms. Plus he had to be extra careful not to penetrate them too deeply in fear of harming the babies.

The girls had an all-night orgy discard at his condo and by the next morning all of his six teams had checked in. They sent encrypted reports that reconnaissance missions were underway.

"All subjects have been spotted?" Joker asked in his own encrypted message replies to the kill teams.

"Affirmative," came back all six responses.

Joker updated Vinny Braga on the status of the mission via encrypted messaging that he had deployed twenty-three of the best killers the Amerikkkan military had ever made and *rest assured*, he wrote, *the fat ladies about to sing.*

We hope you're right, Vinny returned.

Early in the afternoon, to kill some time and to clear his head, he picked up Tithi from her class at NYU Med. He took her out to eat at an expensive French restaurant in Soho, on Mercer St. From there they went to her 10th floor Tribeca loft.

Once inside he was impressed with the transformation. Joker first stepped out onto the private terrace where it was completely brought to life with rows of plants and an intimate outside dining area. While Tithi went to shower and change out of her scrubs, he took in the rest of the decorative changes made by the European-Asian Sensibility decorators.

There was an island kitchen with rift oak cabinetry underneath and all around the top cabinets. The open dining room area had a unique leather wall banquet, a long glass table, and then immaculate wool herringbone linen carpet that brought the brightness out of the room.

In the living area there were walnut floors, Barcelona light fixtures, Calacatta Broghini coffee tables, and a beautiful Euro-Asian infused browns, indigos, and cream colors on the sofas, walks, and area rugs. What hit Joker the most out of the newly decorated loft was the master bedroom. Aside from the beautiful high-end furniture and expensive bed installed in there, Tithi had finalized it with silks and gold finishes to reflect the light during the day or night; there was so much more to look at but he was distracted...

The vision of loveliness appeared out of the bathroom with the sheer silk Chanel teddy on. She had used a blow dryer on her long black hair but her cinnamon colored skin was moist from the hot shower she had taken. She stared at him for a moment before pulling the teddy over her head and dropping it onto the floor. His jaw dropped...

"You shaved it all off," he whispered, noticing her bald little pussy.

Tithi walked past him and he turned to watch as her tight little bubble butt jiggled in that high frequency walk of hers. He saw her pull the covers back and climb between them.

His little Indian Angel was turning into a little devil.

He started to slowly strip for her.

CHAPTER SEVENTEEN

The Tribeca Loft
New York, NY
Thursday, Night

Her breasts, he discovered, where her weak spot. Damp and shiny with his saliva, the brown nipples were hard and standing up like pencil erasers. Her cunt lips were dark and swollen, opening like a blooming flower, the pink in its folds exposed. Clear liquid flowed from her vagina.

"I'm in love with you," Tithi declared out of nowhere.

He stopped sucking her breast and looked adoringly down into her lovely eyes. "I know. And I'm in love with you, too. It was at first sight. I *knew* it."

"But my dad. I'm really close with him," she lamented.

Joker kissed her, tasting her sweet mouth. "Forget that guy you were arranged to marry. Your dad will have to get over it."

Getting into the 69 position, she instantly loved it. Joker knew exactly how to lick her clit and drive her crazy with orgasms. Tithi took his big dick a few inches into her mouth and began sucking sloppily up and down on it, her saliva falling down over the thick stalk like rain. She learned how to move her pussy back and forth in a sensual grind on his mouth while she used her hands to slurp his member in and out of her mouth. Soon their 69 had them rocking the bed as if it were hit by an earthquake.

"I need you now," she breathed as she lay down next to him.

He took hold of her ankles and loved the cute gold toe rings and bracelets she wore. Around her waist was another gold chain, several on her neck, and her wrists were ladened with gold bracelets as were most of her fingers. He loved her pretty feet, kissing each toe before licking and licking in between them. While doing that, Joker massaged her clit to make her even hotter.

"I never thought sex could be so good and I never even had intercourse yet," she whimpered as he sucked her toes and licked her feet. "I like how you love my scent... How you love the taste of me... How you even love my anus. It's so *dirty* but... Such a turn on. And your penis... I only thought porn men had organs so big and long... And *umm, ooh,* your scrotum is very *enlarged*. You will have many babies... *We* will have many babies."

Joker placed a pillow under her buttocks and she spread her exotic brown thighs, giving him access to her private treasure. Moving between her legs and still holding her ankles, he lifted her slightly until his huge member was even with her flowing pussy. He then slowly brought his hips forward so that the bulbous head of his cock rested against her opening.

"Touch it, Princess Tithi," he coached her calmly. "Feel where it's going so you feel no anxiety. It'll only hurt for a second when it breaks through your cherry -- your hymen. It's the small membrane of skin. That's right. Feel how wet you are?"

She nodded. "I'm so horny..."

"Rub your clitoris so you feel pleasure with the pain. Keep rubbing it. Lemme know when it feels mad good, baby."

Using her pussy cream, Tithi masturbated her excited clitoris, prompting her mouth to open in awe as she screamed that it was feeling good. Joker pushed in two inches of his monster as she gasped in pain but kept masturbating. After waiting a moment he fed her a few more inches and felt her hymen pop. Crying out, she held her breath to brace for more pain but it never came.

"Breathe, India, breathe!" he whispered. "That's it! You're a woman now! My woman!"

Joker had every intent of planting his seed in her fertile womb. Tithi kept masturbating, loving the mixture of pain and pleasure she derived from it. Looking down at where they were joined, he was still not all the way inside her tight pussy, so thick it touched both her inner thighs when it entered her.

Within minutes she started making sounds he hadn't heard from her before and she began moving her body forward and back beneath him. His strokes became stronger, faster, and more pronounced. He looked down into her eyes and fucked her now glistening body harder, slowly inching his mammoth dick deeper into her with every stroke.

"Come on, little mama," he commanded her. *"Ride this dick and let me suck your nipples!"*

They flipped over without disconnecting. Joker held tightly onto the full globes of her firm ass cheeks and ran his middle finger down to her sweaty asshole and rubbed circles around it.

"Unnhh, oh my God!" Tithi gasped.

He moved. She moved her body, and his cock almost sliding out of her, then they simultaneously slammed it all the way back in with one quick thrust. Joker was just as amazed as Tithi that she had opened up enough to take all of him. She modified the pace as he suckled her distended nipples and slowly worked a finger into her anus. It all felt divinely delicious and her orgasms came so rapidly that her lips turned white and dry from all the screaming she did.

After a few more of these slow, passionate strokes, he stopped moving. With his cock buried in to the hilt, he looked down at Tithi and said, "Stay still now. I'm goin' to cum. I want you to feel my manhood grow larger and harder. I want you to feel the throbbin' of my big dick as it warns you of my imminent release. I want you to feel my sperm shoot hard against the walls of your fertile womb, keep shooting and filling you till it overflows."

Joker squeezed her buttocks and pushed upwards, biting on her nipples, sucking all over her breasts and her neck, trying to get even deeper inside of her. He groaned and his huge balls contracted as he came; as soon as the first shot of cum spurted she made a yelping sound. He spurted volley after volley of cum inside of her.

"*Ohh, sweet, sweet, India girl,*" he moaned as they kissed. "I've known a lot of women but none have ever pleased me like you! And none ever will."

"A man like you has other women, yes?" She asked him. "You can be honest."

Joker sighed. "I do. And I'll always be honest with you... and I'll always take care of you as long as you are true to me... Faithful... and committed. I have a very unique life and I'm willing to share it with you."

Tithi nodded and gasped as he softened and slid out of her. He looked down at the white sheets and saw small streaks of her vaginal blood on them.

"I'm not naïve," she told him as they cuddled. "I believe you love me... and I love you. In my country, men are allowed the wife and there is no shame in the concubines he had, or the children, but the children cannot become heirs."

He gently kissed her and stroked her sweet smelling hair. "I'm so happy that you gave me your virginity. Lemme ask you somethin'?"

"Anything."

"You ever fantasize about sex with another woman?"

She turned to face him. "It is an abomination in my religion to even consider such a thing... but... when I was in high school, I was shown how to masturbate by a girl."

Joker was all ears. "Really?"

Tithi nodded shyly. "I had never cum so she came up behind

me, put her hands underneath my dress. One in my asscrack and one in the front. She massaged my clitoris and my anus and next thing I knew, my knees buckled and I orgasmed for the first time. But, she moved... and I've fantasized about her ever since."

"Would you ever try it with women?"

"You've opened up something in me that's very liberating," she emphasized. "Let's just say I trust you, baby... Why do you ask?"

"The women I'm involved with know about you and are interested in you. They want you sexually."

Tithi thought about it. "I know I'm young but I'm exceptionally intelligent... You're tryin' to tell me somethin' but you don't trust me."

Joker sat up. "That's not it at all. I'm just workin' on us first."

She sat on top of him. "I know you have *women*. Okay – so what? You've proven yourself to take care of me and there's no denying how much we love each other... I love to be treated like a princess but it's not totally about the money with me. In a year I'll be a medical doctor and make my own money. You know that. But, anyway... I'll be willing to meet your woman or women."

He kissed her softly and more passionately than before.

"However..."

He paused. "However?"

"Yeah," she said, feeling his enormous cock harden against her wet cunt. "How do I have the peace of mind knowing that I can maintain this life you've given me with other females involved?"

He shrugged.

"Well..." She stiffen. "I need you to know. Because you have my virginity, my faith, and I have your live seed inside of my *fertile womb* – remember that?"

"Of course." He ran his fingers affectionately through her illustrious hair.

"I'm a young foreign exchange student in the U.S. alone," she slowly explained. "A year away from achieving my medical license. I gave up my dorm room... what woman in my position wants to be unsure about the ground moving beneath her feet?"

"Security is what you need."

"*Need*, yes," she nodded. "We're not married... What if somethin' happens to you? What will happen to me?"

He reached down on the foot of the bed and pulled out two thick manilla envelopes stuffed with cash. He opened both of them and gave her the rubber banded currency.

"Fifty grand," he informed her. "But this is Amerikkka. Don't go droppin' it in the bank. The Patriot Act demands it be investigated. Especially from a foreigner with brown skin... Place it in a safety deposit box at a bank. You say you need security. Well, so do I. You're a year shy of bein' licensed to practice medicine. How about you ownin' your own business in the health and medicine field?"

"I never thought that far." She was uncertain. "My only focus is becoming a doctor. A general family practice physician. To work at a Mumbai hospital or close to home would get a starting salary of about one hundred twenty five grand. The man I was supposed to marry, a distant cousin, owns a gold mine and other mineral mining companies throughout India. I'm expected to give him sons, honor the Patel family name, and make my father proud."

Joker shook his head. "Hell with that. Fuck wit me and I'll put a million in your pocket a year at *minimum*. Cash is king in this land, India, and it'll help you get citizenship if you want it."

"I want it *now*."

"I'll get you an immigration buyer to help," he promised. "You'd be the crown jewel to any woman I know or ever met. But I want you to make more than a hundred twenty five thou salary... I want you to be a doctor yet why not be more? Own your own practice and create more for us."

"I'm willing to explore options," she decided and held up the cash. "If this falls or fails for any reason... I have rent, food, transportation right here. I just cannot and will not place my education at risk. Now I'm *truly* not insecure of other women in the picture. You showed me the value you place upon me."

She threw the money to the floor and lay back on top of him. The fire was quickly relit and she felt his strong lance pulsating and pounding against her sweet pussy lips.

"Wait," he whispered. "Don't put me back in yet."

"Why?"

"Lemme have a taste of the virgin blood on you and in you, before we wash it away."

The dirtier he was, the more filled with lust she seemed to become. *"Oh my God, that sounds so dirty... but so sexy!"*

"I'll never forget the aroma of you..." he said as he licked hers and his own mixed secretions. *"I'll never forget the taste of you as I swallow you down my throat..."*

He tasted her virginal blood and then climbed up on top of her and wetly kissed the young doctorate student from India.

"Do you taste the blood of your virginity?"

She licked his lips and nodded. "I do... and I taste your sperm mixed in with my blood and I will eternally treasure it. You drive me so crazy with love and lust... that I'll do anything for you."

Joker eased his member deeply inside of her and whispered in her ear while suckling on it. "Imagine me balls deep inside of you... While an extremely hot black girl or white girl... or China girl... has her lips around your clit, tonguing you and me both to blackout orgasms."

"Oh my God, yes," Tithi breathed out her pleasure as he stroked in and out of her tight sheath. "I'll do anything that pleases you."

They made torrid love all through the night.

CHAPTER EIGHTEEN

Team Six
New Orleans, LA
Saturday Evening

A-Son, Mustafa, Blaze, Pooch, and Goliath arrived in New Orleans in separate vehicles that came into the cities that surrounded the one known better as "Nola." For example, they'd flown into Jackson, Mississippi and from there, they traveled incognito into Louisiana/New Orleans via taxi cabs, trains, and buses.

Once there, A-Son entered a used car lot and purchased an old RV with 240,000 miles on it but was assured that it ran well. He paid $4,000 cash for it and placed his own license plate on it.

"That shit looks shaky, son," Blaze commented when A-Son met Team Six outside a bar on Bourbon Street.

"She's a cream puff," A-Son shot back as he opened the creaky door. "It's very clean on the inside but it'll work, for HQ, for now. The guy I bought it from didn't even have a title for it... He tells me: 'Far as I'm concerned, you're buying her for parts.' Only cost four bandz."

Ghost and Joker had allotted each team 10 bands for operation costs but they knew they had to stay off the radar. No hotels and they had to do everything they could to avoid facial recognition on cameras which was why they wore N95 medical masks and sunglasses everywhere they went.

They loaded up their gear onto the RV and drove northeast to an obscure camping ground area along the Mississippi River in La Place. Not far from La Place was Lake Maurepas and the prestigious waterfront mansions in Mandeville which was only a few clicks north from their position.

"We need surveillance vehicles," A-Son said, calling a taxicab to meet him at the entrance of the campground. "C'mon Blaze... Let's go borrow two cars."

"Thought you'd never ask," Blaze said, grabbing his duffel bag and pulling out a screwdriver and a pully. He placed them into a separate, smaller bag and said, "Aight. Let's roll."

While A-Son and Blaze were off hunting for cars to steal, Mustafa pulled out the highly encrypted laptop and set up the satellite/Wi-Fi equipment inside of the RV.

"Ayo, P... Goliath..." He called to them outside where they were building a campfire in the fire pit. The two men came into the RV and sat across the aisle from Mustafa at the dining table. "Call two more taxicabs and go shopping for camping equipment in case the jakes come snoopin' around here. You know the usual survival shit..."

"Sleeping bags, folding chairs, charcoal, lighter fluid, etcetera," Mustafa stated. "One of y'all head off to get food, drinks, coffee, and whatnot."

They exited the campsite. Mustafa checked in on the Dark Net connection with the other teams since Joker had stressed the importance of them trying to synchronize the hits. All the other teams had left encrypted messages for each other to see. Team Six was being asked by the other five teams if they were positioned yet. That pissed Mustafa off.

"Wait. Moved across the fckg contnnt (continent). U moved next door. Just arrived. Recn (recon) not strtd (started). Fckg wait," Mustafa wrote. "Cocky impatient bastards."

When Blaze and A-Son returned with the hot cars, they park them a hundred yards away from base camp. Pooch and Goliath returned lugging huge duffel bags stuffed with supplies. Blaze, A-Son, and Mustafa help them unpack the supplies.

"The other teams are fuckin' rushin' us," Mustafa reported to his squad as they stood around the campfire cooking hot dogs over the flames.

"They ain't have to travel a thousand miles," Pooch reasoned.

"Exactly," Mustafa agreed as he put his Ballpark frank on a hot dog bun and then dressed it up with ketchup, mustard, and relish.

"We ain't trying to hear that shit," Blaze dismissed it.

However, Mustafa showed them the files of the mafia chief they had to assassinate. There was a detailed map and aerial view photos of the property from Google Earth. There was also a stack of ten photos they reviewed again.

"This granddaughter of his..." Goliath pointed at the picture. "She lives with him at the mansion and attends a private school right there in Mandeville: *St. Peter's Prep.* No mother, no father – why, we don't know. But I'm willing to bet he picks her up."

Mustafa logged in on the school's website and nodded. "Pandemic rules restricts the kids to three in-person school days: Monday, Tuesday, and Friday. Virtual studies on Thursday; off on Wednesday, Saturday, and Sunday."

Mustafa pulled up Google Earth aerial images of Saint Peter's Catholic Preparatory School. "Okay, here we go."

A-Son was calling the shots so he spoke. "We have to get it crackin'. We start recon on the house since it sits up on a hill apart from others in the community. There's a *higher* hill diagonally from the home across Lake Maurepas."

"Yeah," Pooch pointed to the map on the monitor. "It's a

hundred seventy yards across the lake. If he steps out the front door I can take that shot and it's back to New Yitty for us."

"There's a forest line there," A-Son highlighted the fact. "We need one man to camp out in a tree over there. We also have to get these two bombs underneath his favorite car – a Gray Hummer."

"A ninety-thousand dollar Hummer," Mustafa added for good measure. "He drives the best."

"We gotta get Pooch over to the lake tonight," A-Son said, studying the GPS coordinates. "There's a road nearby. Take the car, hide it in the forest, camouflage it... So if and when the order comes down and you have the shot then take it, Pooch."

"Don't worry," Pooch assured him. "I'll blend into the trees I'll be perched in better than a squirrel."

"Goliath," A-Son looked across the fire at the big man. "You go with him. Y'all gotta figure out how you'll get across that lake to strap the Hummer up with these fireworks."

"You sure you want to send this tall ass mufucka on the Giatorre Property?" Pooch joked.

"I can do it," Goliath emphasized. "I've done special cover ops nearly all my career. My height is not an impediment, it's a *strength*."

"Pooch and Goliath are dismissed then," A-Son ordered. "Finish your meals."

———

Lake Maurepas
Late Evening

Pooch and Goliath were in position across Lake Maurepas by midnight. Pooch located the ideal place to hide and perch thirty feet up inside of a giant hundred year old Sycamore tree.

Goliath, careful to stay inside of the tree line, went off to scout the shoreline. Dressed in all black tactical gear, he moved along quickly but cautiously because he did not know the terrain. There could be deadly traps, silent alarms, or even cameras for that matter as part of Nicholas Giatorre's security apparatus.

Goliath, wearing top of the line U.S. Army issued infrared goggles, forged stealthily ahead until he came upon a boat dock with a cedar wood pier that extended seventy-five yards out over the lake.

"Kill Box One Alpha to Blackbird, over," Goliath radioed Pooch.

"Blackbird, over."

"Found a full line marina that extends nearly halfway across. Appears to be non-exclusive to our friend but to the entire community. Kill Box One Alpha will take his chances, over."

"Godspeed, over and out."

Goliath made sure the C-4 bombs and his other gear was protected inside of a waterproof sack which he attached to his ankle. He waded into the water and after the initial shock of the cold, he ignored it and began the 250-foot swim to the marina. Fortunately, it was a lake in the South and not one in the north. There was no danger of hypothermia setting in because the water wasn't that cold.

When he reached the end of the pier he climbed up the wooden underbelly and used his upper body strength to scale up to the edge and pull himself up to the surface. He opened up the waterproof safety bag and redressed in dry gear. He checked the bombs and saw that they were dry. Once he had everything else secured in his backpack, Goliath checked his fully automatic modified AR-15, extra extended clips, then he used infrared binoculars to scan the entire marina.

Moments later, the tall giant moved on past the fancy speed-boats, sailboats, and yachts that were docked alongside the marina. He walked by a 17-foot sailboat that had a light on the cabin below deck and it sounded like a couple was inside having sex. There was more late night activity heard on a yacht dock closer to the shore-line. There was also some sort of party going on inside.

Goliath carried off the pier before he was spotted and walked across a cobblestone walkway. He scaled the high wrought iron gate which surrounded the opulent number $15 million waterfront mansion. Goliath removed his trusty M9 Beretta and screwed on its suppressor. The grounds were well lit so he tried using the manicured rose bushes and trees for cover as he stalked towards the hexagon-shaped parking area in front of the main entrance of the house.

He spotted the fancy gray Hummer that Don Nicholas "Nicky" Giatorre loved to be seen in. Goliath was a heartless soldier who survived three wars by pure guts and instinct so he didn't hesitate. He was already there so he crouched as low as he could and made his way to the Hummer.

He shimmied beneath it and attached one of the C-4 bombs underneath the center where the primary passengers compartment was. Then, just as he was about to attach the other bomb closer to where the driver seat was, he heard the sounds of men walking and talking. He froze and readied his pistol for firing because getting caught was not an option.

Two pairs of feet walk by, entered a Lincoln Navigator, and drove away. Goliath breathed easier and worked fast to complete the job of planting the backup bomb. Once he was done he looked around to make sure he was not spotted before heading back to the marina.

As he was – once again – stripping, he heard people talking and laughing as a white couple in their thirty's emerged from the sailboat he'd heard them making love inside of earlier. They walked out onto the pier and noticed Goliath standing there with his speedos on and the black waterproof backpack on the ground next to him.

"Excuse me, sir," the man called out to Goliath.

Goliath didn't hesitate. He turned around and started shooting. He shot the woman in the face and her lover in the chest. They both fell backwards, their bodies slamming backwards into the pier.

"Shit!" Goliath muttered as he rushed towards them. He

finished the man off with another shot to his temple. *More fuckin' work!*

He now moved with desperation as he first lifted the man up off the ground and shoved his body back into the sailboat. Next, he picked up the limp corpse of the woman and threw her onto the sailboat next to her lover. Goliath retrieved his backpack and hopped onto the vessel with them.

Taking a much needed breather he scanned the marina and the other boats docked there for any movement. The highly trained assassin hauled the bodies downstairs and an idea struck him.

He prepared the boat for sailing out of the marina.

CHAPTER NINETEEN

Don Frank Braga
Chicago, Illinois
Sunday Morning

Vinnie let the black Chrysler 300 come to a stop outside of *La Italia Cafe & Restorante* on 45th and Racine in Chicago before he dashed out into the relentless rain and hopped into the back seat.

"So," Don Braga said.

"So," Vinnie repeated. "No new updates other than its all imminent."

Don Braga, seated next to his brother in the back seat, said to his driver, "Hey, Olivio, go get a coffee or somethin' will ya?"

"Sure, boss," the driver replied and exited the vehicle.

"You don't think this thing is takin' too long?" Frank asked in a deeply concerned voice.

Vinnie thought it over. "Are ya kiddin' me or what? Before I knew them guys, I hated 'em. I wanted 'em dead. But then you made me realize their value to us. C'mon, Frankie. Don't worry."

Frank shook his head. "Don't worry? I'll tell you what I'm

worried about... *Lombardo. DiGiorgio. Gambino. Santino. Dellacroce. Giatorre...* If *one* goes wrong we're fuckin' dead. Just *one*."

"Now you got my heart beatin'," Vinnie accused him. "Jesus, Mary, Paul, and Joseph!"

"Yeah," Frank nodded. "That's who we'll need if this goes South."

———

Lake Maurepas
Dawn – Sunday

Using the enormous steel anchor to add weight to the two bodies stuffed inside of the large white canvas sack, he located on the rear deck of the boat, Goliath used nylon twine to tie it up tight and then dropped it overboard before sailing the vessel north of Pooch's position and radioed him.

"*Kill Box One Alpha to Blackbird, over,*" Goliath called to him.

"*Blackbird*, over," Pooch came back.

"*Ran into two problems,*" Goliath said. "*Had to clean up, over.*"

"*And the fireworks? Over.*"

"*Mission accomplished, over.*"

There was a brief pause.

"*Return to the hide post,*" Pooch told him. "*Contact base camp with the news, over.*"

Goliath contacted A-Son via radio and informed him of the night's progress. He sounded pleased about it and in turn, informed Goliath that the rest of the team were already positioned at St. Peter's Preparatory School in Mandeville.

"*I have to contact the others to let them know we have reason to believe this alligator hunt is coming to a close, over,*" A-Son told him.

Meanwhile, Goliath went down into the hull of the boat and attached a C-4 door charge to the floor. He then stripped and packed away his weapons and gear in the waterproof backpack.

After setting off the charge, he dove into the water and swam the 100 yards back to shore. When he got there he looked back at the boat and it had already began descending down into its watery grave. The mercenary hurried and dressed as dawn broke out across the massive lake.

He was at least a mile away from where Pooch was posted. Once dressed he ran all the way to the tree where his partner was and opened up the backpack. Goliath readied the detonator which was programmed into both bombs as well as the two burner phones which were also programmed into the bombs.

Knarf had earlier explained at the EIE HQ in Nyack: *"This is to make sure nothing goes wrong. The detonator backs ups the call phones and the call phones back up the detonator. When it's time, use the detonator by pressing both buttons at the same time. It should go **BOOM!!!** But if something goes awry... Used the call phones. Each bomb has a burner attached to the C-4 charge on a one second timer. Use those two burners to call those two and after the first ring – **BOOM!!!!"***

Goliath waited for instructions from A-Son.

Indian Sun Condos
Dawn – Sunday

Joker sat in his study with his designated encrypted communications coordinators: Uzenna, Diane, and Leah. They were monitoring the live messages as they were exchanged to and from via the dark web. There was stress and excitement in their Indian-Sun office study now:

"Team One Report: Success with fireworks connection; locked in on sub (subject) *locale,"* Diane read aloud. "That's out of New Jersey, Pat Lombardo, Bonanno Crime Family."

"Tell 'em standby," Joker ordered. "Next."

"Team Two Report: Success with the connection but sub is hospitalized

with pneumonia. Easy target. We can go in, give a hot shot, and be done," Uzenna read next. "This is Victor DiGiorgio of the Colombo Crime Family in Manhattan."

Joker nodded. "Tell them to administer that hot shot. It'll look like natural causes at least for a few months."

Uzenna sent the order to N9NE, Monk, and Caesar to get it over with.

"Team Three report: Had to follow to Florida on vacay but success with attachment on lux rental; Fam on beach in luxe bungalow," Leah rattled off the details. "Carlo Gambino, III, of the Gambino Crime Fam., is sunning himself out on the open beach it seems."

"That's War, Eddie, Broliks, and Bible, right?" Joker ask them.

"That's correct," Leah said.

"Tell 'em line up the shot but standby," he said. "Team Four..."

"Team Four Report: No success in attachment because use of several different vehicles... However, have eyes on college age mysteries he sees each day at same time, one bodyguard," Diane relayed the message. "That's from Emanuel Santino of the Genovese fam in Queens."

Joker rubbed his clean-shaven face. "Tell Chief, Knarf, Ghost, and Rogue to get ready."

"Team Five Report: attachment success; awaiting orders," Uzenna read off the brief message. "Lucchese Crime Family's Paul Dellacroce of Brooklyn."

"That's..." Joker sounded uncertain.

"Breach, Knox, Bone, and Colombiana," Uzenna reminded him.

Joker nodded. "Tell 'em stand by... And tell A-Son to let his team loose. They have the green light."

"Team Two, Team Six... you have the go," Uzenna wrote and sent the encrypted message to all teams. *"One, Three, Four, and Five please standby."*

Joker thought it through for several minutes more until he realized the impossibility of synchronizing the hits. The best he could do was to have his teams hit these bastards hard and to hit them before the news could reach the others that the hunters had become the hunted.

Uzenna, Leah, and Diane nervously looked at their man. They knew what he was thinking.

"Tell them all to go and to go now!" He stood up to emphasize. "We got to go hard and fast because we can't afford them to be spooked and for any of them to beef up security. Go, go, go!"

Uzenna sent a message to all teams.

CHAPTER TWENTY

The Nikki Giatorre Hit
Mandeville, LA
Monday Morning

By the time Pooch and Goliath received word that they had the green light to kill Nicholas Giatorre, it was already day break. Goliath and Pooch moved away from base camp as quickly as they could and hustled their way back to their camouflaged vehicle.

They drove the two and two-thirds mile drive around to the lakefront mansion just as −

"Holy *fuck*!!" Pooch snapped as the Hummer barreled right past them! "That's them!"

Goliath was driving. He made a U-turn and stepped on it, putting the sun visor down because the morning sun was beaming so brightly that it nearly blinded him.

"You got confirmed sighting?" Goliath needed to be sure.

"One-hundred fuckin' percent!"

It took a minute but the 2009 Toyota Camry caught up to the Hummer and Goliath confirmed the license plate number. He went a step further and drove past the top-of-the-line luxury SUV to see if he could get a better look...

And there he was. A medium built Italian man with dark hair that was graying around the edges. He actually drove his own vehicle. There was a bodyguard or two which sat in the rear compartment but their faces were obscured by partially opened windows.

"The little girl's in there!" Pooch whispered suddenly.

"Okay," Goliath said as the Hummer powered on past a set of train tracks. "Grab the detonators, Pooch."

But Pooch struggled with that. "And blow up that little girl, too?" He refused to retrieve the detonators.

Goliath couldn't believe what he was hearing from a fellow assassin. "Are you fuckin' *crazy?*"

"We killed enough kids over there, G," Pooch growled as he reached between the seats into his duffel bag in the back. "Let's have a little dignity and save *this* one, alright?"

"Okay..." Goliath muttered quietly.

Then, as Pooch readied his AR-15, a silenced **"PPHHFFTT!!"** sound burst from the Beretta Goliath held in his left hand. The shot hit Pooch in the left temple and pieces of brain and skull matter splattered onto the window and doorway of the Camry.

"In case you ain't know, Pooch," Goliath said to his lifeless comrade. "We ain't the good guys anymore."

Goliath pulled the Camry over to the side of the road and reached back into his backpack. Placing it onto his lap, he opened it and removed the burner phones that were programmed into the bombs. He pulled up the speed dial function on both phones and "called" into the phones attached to the bombs.

Goliath heard the explosion from where he sat a mile behind the Hummer. He then saw the plumes of black smoke ascend high into the clear morning sky. Goliath shoved Pooch's body down as far as it would go to the floor before he took off to examine the bomb scene.

When he drove slowly by, the trained killer scanned the

wreckage and observed that the Hummer had been obliterated and turned into a molten hot ball of flames. The explosion had sent the engine flying fifty yards into the cattle field to the left. There were three charred bodies strewn about in different locations with one that appeared to be that of a small child.

Goliath knew then that the mission was complete. He returned to base camp in La Place to meet up with Mustafa, A-Son, and Blaze.

"We gotta pack up and go," Goliath said quickly.

"Where's Pooch?" Blaze asked him.

"He's in the car," Goliath stated. "Dead."

Mustafa, A-Son, and Blaze walked over to the Camry to see for themselves.

"What the fuck happened out there?" A-Son needed to know.

Goliath explained everything and then added, "No way I coulda let him fuck up the hit and face Red later," he shook his head vehemently. "No fuckin' way."

"The Mississippi River is closed by so..." Mustafa shrugged. "Let's scrub it clean, dump the body, the car... And go home."

A-Son looked at Pooch and shook his head.

———

The Indian Sun Condos
Monday Evening

Joker took a deep breath and smiled at Uzenna, Leah, and Diane. "We did it! We fuckin' did it!"

He affectionately hugged and kissed each of them and ordered them to pack up all the computers, hard drives, and communications equipment used in the transmissions to the teams.

"Everything must burn," he told them as he left the room.

Julia, Valerie, Iani, and Romie tailed along with him to the EIE/TPP warehouse. The front sliding security gate got stuck and they had to get out of the sleek blue Cadillac truck and push it the rest of the way open.

Once inside of the office Joker opened up a secure backroom that was situated next to the bathroom and underneath an industrial steel shelf was the floor safe. He used two green duffel bags, closed, and locked up everything and returned to the Indian Sun Condominium tower in which they lived.

Back inside of the office-study he saw that the girls had boxed up everything and he helped them tape up the boxes and carry them out into the living room. Joker returned to the office and summoned all thirteen of his women to assist.

"Each of these are bundled in ten thousand dollar stacks," he instructed the ladies. "Please place thirty of them in each brown paper bag."

"Oh, that ain't hard." Iani giggled.

They made quick work of the 23 bags of $300K to be paid to each hitter.

Joker sent an encrypted message to Don Braga via his laptop: *"Success all across the board!"*

Don Braga wrote back: *"Your success is our bridge to the future. NOW you're my friend."*

Joker showed Uzenna, Leah, and Diane the message and they smiled.

"Have an enormous soul food feast catered to us," Joker beamed. He was very happy. "Bust out all the best wine and liquor for our crew. They just cemented for all of us in this room a very lucrative and power future. And because y'all been so patient with me, Uz, Leah, and Diane... I'm sendin' y'all on a vacation trip to Las Vegas where you'll stay in your own luxury suites at the world famous Mandalay. All expenses will be paid on my Black Card *except* gambling. You'll each have ten grand in spending money so... have fun."

The girls were squealing with their own brand of excitement.

They knew that with the babies on the way, there would likely be no such fun ahead for awhile. And Uzenna said as much.

"Babe," Joker told her. "We'll be good. When y'all get back, we're lookin' for the ideal mansion on the lake in or around Chicago millionaires... and we'll hire an army of nurses and nannies to care for y'all and the babies. If we can find it, maybe even a luxury apartment buildin', so many of you can have your own separate piece of the Amerikkkan pie."

"We'd all still be in the same building?" Julia wanted to clarify. "But have our own separate place, our own bathrooms..?"

"Just an idea y'all can explore," he reasoned. "It's one thing for us to share three condos or live in some huge mansion with fifty or sixty rooms but another to have your own space and quiet with a baby."

Iani ordered the catered food to be delivered by 8:00 PM which was short notice for Sylvia's Soul Food Restaurant in Manhattan. When she offered to pay triple with a $1000 tip for the caterers, they agreed to prioritize the delivery.

And none too soon because the kill teams started to arrive one after the other.

CHAPTER TWENTY-ONE

The Indian Sun Condos
Late Monday Eve

Each brown paper bag was marked with a name and taped shut with the thick piece of masking tape. As each of the male and female assassins entered Joker's house, they were immediately paid for their work. By 11:00 PM the celebratory dinner party was in full swing. Joker walked through his luxurious condo taking inventory of the teams that had made it back home so far:

Boo, Divine, and Bushwacker of Team One.

N8NE, Monk, and Caesar of Team Two.

War, Eddie, Broliks, and Bible of Team Three.

Knox, Bonecrusher, La Colombiana, and Breach of Team Five.

"Team Six ain't back yet," Ghostman interrupted Joker's thoughts. Ghostman handed Joker a glass of whiskey on the rocks.

"A-Son, Mustafa, Blaze, Goliath, and Pooch," Joker acknowledged. "They had to travel far but they bought an RV to camp out of while in Nola. Guess that's they transpo back. Bad news, though."

Ghostman looked at him.

"A-Son sent a transmission that they lost one while they were down there," Joker informed him.

"Which one?"

Joker shrugged. "He didn't say. Only that it would be best if it's all explained face to face."

Uzenna went to the front door and opened it after receiving a text message. She was greeted by what looked like at endless line of nicely dressed young women and at least three older women who look to be in their late 30s and early 40s. The men all stopped what they were doing and all eyes shifted to the lovely new faces.

Joker observed that his thirteen women all hugged and enthusiastically greeted each of the women.

"Who are they?" Ghostman questioned Joker.

"Your guess is as good as mine," Joker shrugged.

"Everyone!" Uzenna called out after she used the remote to pause the music. "Lemme introduce to y'all some friends of ours that we've known for a long time. I know others were recruited by my other sisters like Coral, Brittani, Val, Eden, and down the line. When Red put out a call to recruit military and mercenary comrades, we put our brains together and did the same. These girls, like us, were in various situations, strip clubs, dopers, the streets, etcetera. Some have kids that had they left with family or loved ones while they investigate my offer... Well, the offer of the thirteen. We sent them plane tickets and pocket money..."

"And rooms at Holiday Inn," Eden quipped.

Uzenna pointed at Joker. "That's Joker Red — my husband and king. He's the big boss around these parts."

"Hello, ladies," Joker nodded, standing next to Uzenna.

They all said *hello* back to him.

"I know there's a lot of them to know," Uzenna said. "But this is Destinee, Crystal, Pollyanna, Avi, Mika, Olivia, Lady, Kitten, Laura, Sinnamon, Yadi, Chanel, Cheekie, Tiera, Sherri, Jayda, Tiffani, Journee, and Stormm."

Coral introduced the girls she knew. "This is Kandi, Rosa, Nellie, Yolie, and Patricia."

Valerie introduced the three older women. "Cat, Bell, and Gigi. They looked out for some of us before they made a break for it."

Brittany introduced the last of them. "These are some of the most wanted magical acrobatic chicks in the game period... Mackenzie, Esmeralda Cartegena, Lexie, Carla DeLeon, Isabella Caronna, and Jessica Cicero."

"So," Ghostman said, stepping forward. "I count thirty-four of you. Of thirty... Only Cat, Bell, and Gigi no longer dance?"

The women all nodded.

"Carla, Isabel, and Jessica," Joker called out to them. "Y'all are Italian?"

They all nodded.

"Y'all speak it?"

They nodded again.

The one called Cheekie, a pretty black girl with an ass like Serena's, said, "We didn't come to New York to dance. We came to do something bigger. That's what Yu, Romi, and nem said."

"Ghostman only asked if youse danced, sweetie," Joker told her. "We don't have nowhere for y'all to dance. However, we might need to use y'all's skills to reach a higher purpose... but you won't be paid no funky ass ones to do it. So, calm your little cute ass down."

Ghostman opened up his brown paper bag and removed the 300K. "You ever see three hundred thou, baby?"

Cheekie looked at the money and shook her head.

"This condo you in?" Ghostman went on as he stood in front of her. "Half a million... And we own three others on this same floor. And none of this shit is worth dog spit compared to what we really got poppin'. No one brought you here to play little league baseball."

"Easy, Ghostman," Uzenna said to him. "A little bit TMI. Plus, I'm running this show over here with these bitches."

Ghostman threw his hands up. "My bad, Lady Boss."

"Cheekie, you always did have a big mouth," Uzenna checked

her ass. "You know how to talk yourself out of the life of luxury. Hey, Iani."

"Yeah, sis." Iani walked over.

"Call this bitch an Uber," Uzenna ordered. "And book her on a flight back to Mississippi."

"Wait, Uzenna!" Cheekie complained. "Are you serious?"

"Rogue, La Colombiana..." Uzenna called them over. "Do me a favor?"

"Don't worry about it," Ghostman volunteered. "I have to head out to B-K, anyway. I'll hit the Belt Parkway over to the Grand Central Parkway and take her to La Guardia myself. Come on Cheekie." Ghostman escorted her out.

"Okay, ladies," Uzenna stated. "Does anyone else wanna talk fly to my husband, me, or any of us? Especially when you were all *told* you'd not be forced into sex, dancing, or anything else?"

The women kept quiet.

"Right now, I just want you to relax and mingle" Uzenna urged them. "Enjoy the food, the drinks, the good lookin' men. Don't worry about work – we got work."

"TPP, babe," Joker reminded her.

"We have two stores," she explained. "Called The Paper Place. One in Rockland County... the other in Westchester County. We are expandin' our empire and will need three or four to run each TPP store. There's a lot we have to train you for in TPP... And then we are buyin' hotels from New York to Chicago. This ain't the *Make A Wish Foundation* or no *United Way*... We play championship ball up here. Most of youse will need to work in legit spots – our stores, our hotels, whatever. But there's more to it. You'll earn a legit check on the surface but under the surface, cash is gonna come with more risk."

"That's enough for you now, though," Joker interjected. "They're all at the Holiday Inn you said?"

Eden nodded. "*I* said, daddy. Yeah. They're at the one next to La Guardia."

"Cancel the rooms," Joker ordered Eden. "Does any of y'all wish to leave? If you do, I'll buy you a ticket to wherever you wish with five hundred in your pocket."

The women all looked at each other, shaking their heads to decline the offer.

"They got kids they want to bring up," Uzenna told him.

"Y'all get it, right?" Iani asked the women. "We ain't moving Girl Scout cookies, you know? These cats are the heavy hitters."

A beautiful Latina with more curves than Cardi B and J-Lo put together raised her hand. "How heavy?"

"Top of the food chain," Iani told her.

"And you are again?" Joker inquired from the round-face darling with light brown eyes.

"Yolie Santana," she answered.

"There's a nice Hyatt Hotel close by," Joker told them. "Baby, put five hundred dollars in everyone's pockets and get them the best rooms they got. Train and fill the TPP positions ASAP because we headin' out to Chi-Town soon."

Uzenna went to the master bedroom and retrieved the cash she was ordered to give the new females. She passed out $500 to each one and then she called the Hyatt to make reservations. She was able to get an entire floor of luxury suites and reported the news to the 33 ladies.

Everyone ate the food, had their fill of drinks, and loved the socialization. All the male hitters from the five teams paired off with fifteen of the new girls and followed them to their rooms at the Hyatt. When it looked like Bible would be left out to dry, Joker got Yolie Santana's attention.

"Hey, baby," he whispered to her. "Why don't you take my man Bible to the hotel with you? The nigga ain't had a woman in years."

She looked over at him. "I can see why. He's a monster."

Joker nodded. "But no one in the world is more loving or loyal. You can't do wrong doin' me a favor."

"You owe me *big*, man," she told Joker before walking over to Bible.

It took her some time but she finally persuaded Bible to leave with her. By the moment the sun had started to come up, everyone had exited.

"Finally!" Joker said, yawning. "Now, I can sleep!"

CHAPTER TWENTY-TWO

Most of Cheekie's savagely bruised and beaten body was buried beneath the rocks and dirt. All that was left to see of her was the right side of her face. Her dyed red hair was strewn across her forehead and eyes. Ghostman used the shovel to cover up the rest of the nude girl's body inside of the grave.

When he was done, he picked up the plastic Ziploc bag that held all of her teeth which he'd pulled out himself using a hammer and an icepick. Also inside the bag was her fingers. He wanted to be sure that if the body was ever dug up that dental records nor finger prints could ever come back that a match was found.

He was at a construction site in Nyack where dozens of new homes were being built. He and Cheekie had never even left this small city. Ghostman charmed and seduced her while promising that he would take care of her. They had started out by having blazing hot sex in the rear seat of his Cadillac SUV as she'd orgasmed beneath his relentless pounding thrust while choking her.

Cheekie had managed to knee him in the balls and beat him with her fists. He went ballistic after that. Ghostman had beaten her recklessly, without mercy. He had taken her out of the car and that's when he had savagely beaten her with a hammer until she died.

He grabbed an icepick and hammer and removed her teeth. And he'd used a knife to remove her fingers. After burying Cheekie, he'd left the construction site and returned to the Indian Sun Condos where he flushed the fingers and teeth down the toilet.

Without another thought about her, Ghostman bagged up his clothes, showered, and fell into a needed sleep.

———

Indian Sun Condos
Nyack, NY
Tuesday Evening

Joker didn't wake up until almost 5:00 PM and by 5:15 PM he was entering the EIE condo. He had been told by Uzenna that A-Son had called earlier but she refused to wake him.

A-Son, Mustafa, Blaze, and Goliath were in the condo's media-game room sitting around playing the *PlayStation* with Rogue and La Colombiana sipping on drinks nearby.

"Everybody still at the hotel?" Joker asked as he sat in a plush black leather recliner.

"Except Ghost," Colombiana replied as she sat next to Joker. She wore a pink T-shirt that showed off her nice round tits and protruding nipples. She had on form fitting Daisy Dukes which boasted not only her Colombian ass, hips, and delectable pussy print but beautiful long toned legs with sexy tattoos on them with very pretty feet and toes. She boldly ran her left hand softly down the back of his wavy head and neck. "Hi, Red."

"Ola mi amor," he said to her and turn back to A-Son. "So who the *fuck's* gonna tell me why Pooch is fuckin' dead?!"

"I will, sir," Goliath said.

"Drop the 'sir' shit. We ain't in the field."

"Yes, sir, I mean —" Goliath stopped himself. "We were in pursuit of the target's vehicle when we made a pass to ID the occupants. I had to be certain. I made the usual ID and directed Pooch to ready the detonators but he refused."

"Fuckin' refused?" Joker asked as Ghostman appeared shirtless and sat down by himself on another sofa.

"There was a tender aged girl in the vehicle," Goliath shrugged. "He put the entire mission in jeopardy. He went on about all the kids we killed in Afghanistan, Syria... I made the decision right there that I wasn't going to be responsible for blowin' this mission. So I pulled my sidearm out and ... He expired."

There was silence.

Until Ghostman burst out laughing. "Damn!"

"Ain't that the shit that got Tony Montana killed in *Scarface?*" Rogue said. "Sosa took that as betrayal and murdered Tony's whole crew."

Joker looked at the raven-haired Air Force fighter pilot. "Yeah... Goliath, you saved the mission. I owe you one."

Joker Red stood up to shake the giant's hand.

"You got a woman?" Joker asked Goliath.

Goliath shook his head. "Women take time. And money. And I have a mortgage."

"Well you have three hundred K now," Joker informed him. "As far as women, I want all y'all to head over to the Hyatt and text me your rooms. Come on over to get your money, secure it, and go. I need everyone to have fun and be rested for what's next."

A-Son, Mustafa, Blaze, and Goliath collected their $300K from Joker's condo and headed over to the Hyatt. Once he had their room numbers, Joker used a high-end escort service based out of Manhattan to send eight of their most beautiful women to the Hyatt in Nyack.

Don Braga and Joker spoke later that night over burner phones.

"I like your style more and more," Braga complemented Joker. *"Anyone else woulda taken da cash and ran."*

"Cash is easy," Joker said as he spoke in the presence of his thirteen women. He had Frank on speaker phone. *"Legitimizing it... That's the power."*

"So here's what I propose," Frank started. *"I have six big ones of your cash. You and your buyer meet with my stock brokers and investment bunkers so you can be invested. I'll use my influence and the influence of my associates to secure your company a loan that will make your head spin."*

Joker sat forward on the sofa inside of their living area. *"A loan like what? And... TPP, LLC., and EIE, Inc., are wound up tight. To keep the IRS off our ass we have maximized our loan capacity."*

"You can have any loan you say you want," Frank assured him. *"You just need the collateral and I have companies -- for example, my Italian wine company -- that can sell you shares too and you can use the shares as collateral. I own dozens of companies that can sign over shares to your companies and you can prove that you have holdings valued at or over the value of the loan or loans. However, you'll be held liable for the taxes on the transfer of shares. But they won't be your shares. They'll only be on loan for a time... to help manipulate loaners into giving you massive loans."*

Joker was trying to take it all in. *"Isn't that fraud?"*

Braga chuckled. *"It's only fraud if they can **prove** it. One way they can do that is for you not to invest the money into hotels and other investments as you claim."*

"What kinds of loans?" Eden whispered into his ear.

"What loan amounts can we get?" Joker asked him.

"Fifty to seventy-five million," Braga guessed. *"Maybe more."*

Joker stood up, barely able to contain his excitement. ***"Legitimate dollars** across the board?"*

"Yeah, but I have to tell you," Don Braga stated in his raspy voice in Chicago Italian accent. *"The wolves will be salivatin' at your breakfast table, lunch, suppa, and nippin' at the feet of your babies for cash like that. Everyone will have their hand out, includin' me. **Especially** me. I have confidence that you'll cover the costs of legitimacy. It's not free."*

Joker waited.

"Put it like this." Braga paused. *"For every washed ten mill you get, you'll be paying' me an extra three million."*

"That is expensive," Joker acknowledged.

"It's expensive to be rich," Braga told him. *"But it costs even more to be poor."*

"Tell me about it."

"There's a bright side," Braga reminded him. *"If you are successful out here with the other job as you were with the other period... Sheesh! Even the sky won't be high enough for you."*

After he hung up the phone, he turned to the girls. **"We 'bout to be legit!"**

"On every *million*..." Uzenna emphasize. "We gotta pay three hundred grand to clean. So, you understand. On top of that we're responsible for interest, taxes, insurance, mortgages, the loans themselves, all of our other loans and bills."

"Medical," Valerie pointed to her baby bump.

Joker laughed. "Y'all worry too much. Once we land the loan, we'll be debt-free. And the cash that'll come from the mid-west meth operation, our dark web ops, East Coast ops, and prisons will be astounding."

"There's no holding us back now!" Iani felt the excitement. "I see the big vision."

"Y'all heard it yourselves," Joker said as he pulled Valerie and Eden to him. "We need to *move*. Train the girls for the stores... Find us an exclusive place to live in Chi-Town where we'll all be solid."

Uzenna was already way ahead of him.

CHAPTER TWENTY-THREE

Crystal Lake, IL
Tuesday Morning

A week later Uzenna and Coral arrived in Chicago with most of the new girls: Mika, Olivia, Lady, Kitten, Laura, Sinnamon, Yadi, Chanel, Tiera, Sherri, Jayda, Tiffani, Journee, Nya, Stormm, Kandi, Rosa, Nellie, Yolie, Patricia, Mackenzie, Esmeralda, Lexie, Carla, Isabella, and Jessika.

Cat, Bell, and Gigi, the three older women, were being trained to manage and run The Paper Place in Nyack and New Rochelle.

The first thing they did when they disembarked from their flight at 8:00 AM was load up on a chartered luxury bus that took them to Crystal Lake which was east of North Chicago. There, they were ushered inside of a massive 18,000 square foot Palatial mansion the owners had rented out on AirBNB for 10,000 per night. It had 64 rooms and came with the full staff of maids, cooks, security, and grounds keepers.

"It's beautiful!" Yolie squealed in her excitement.

They all got situated in their rooms while Uzenna made a phone

141

call to Don Braga's real estate broker. Uzenna and Coral were picked up in a Mercedes stretch limousine and driven to an all-white brick eight story apartment building on West Lawrence Avenue in the city. Uzenna knew the apartments were luxurious masterpieces but it was the parking in the area that made her turn it down. It was far from efficient.

The next two buildings they were shown, she fell in love with. The twin white marble and stucco structures were constructed for executives and the well-off. They were each six stories high, each had multiple penthouse units on the top floor, plenty of parking, swimming pools outside, basement gyms, and much more.

"*These* are on the market?" Uzenna asked, mildly surprised as she was led inside of the first floor apartment. "They're beautiful!"

"Yes, they are," Vanessa Chiabella, the slim Italian broker, assured. "The pandemic forced the corporation that owns these architectural marvels into bankruptcy."

After seeing the penthouse Uzenna made her decision. "I want them both. What's the price tag?"

"Prior to the bankruptcy – *ten million*," Vanessa informed them. "Now the bank is selling them off for *four million*."

"Wow," Coral laughed.

"Sixty total units," Uzenna stated. "Let's do it."

Once the deal was completed Uzenna and Coral returned to the Crystal Lake palace. They met with local decorators on *Zoom* who promised to sit with them the following day.

As the night wore down Uzenna reported to Joker Red about her amazing discovery.

"I got all the photos," he told her. "There's thirty apartments in each building?"

"Yeah," she replied. "For one person it's really a lot of room. There's three penthouse units on the top floor of each building. There's terraces. The penthouses are *approximately* the size of our Nyack home."

"How's the baby?"

She smiled at that. "I'm fine. The baby is fine but I feel he or she is getting impatient."

"You're a warrior, love."

———

The "Twin Towers"
Chicago, Ill.

The decorators moved at warp speed to help her decorate her and Joker's penthouse. Uzenna also had them create a nursery while she used various websites such as *instacart.com* and *Amazon.com* to stock the kitchen and refrigerator shelves with food and other supplies.

She did the same thing with all the other 29 units in her building. She made sure they had food, bathroom supplies, bedroom, living room, dining room furniture, and other basics. Coral was by her side all of the way as well as the 26 new girls.

"These are really nice!" Yolie said as she and Uzenna let an Amazon deliveryman bring several boxes into one of the 5th floor apartments. "Is this where we'll live?"

"Not in this buildin'," Uzenna answered her. "I want you all over in the next buildin'."

Uzenna and Coral waited to gather all the girls together.

"This buildin' is reserved for my husband and my sister-wives," Uzenna informed them as they stood inside her penthouse apartment. "For any of y'all that's slow... All thirteen of us are with Joker Red and we are all pregnant with his children. Anyway, the only women living in this buildin' is us and EIE soldiers. I know some of y'all started romances with them – we'll see where that goes."

"Speaking of which," the Italian brunette named Isabella said with a smile. "How was that big brute you were with Yolie?"

Even Uzenna and Coral wanted to know that.

Yolie laugh shyly. "I thought he'd crushed me but he turned out to be the most sensitive man."

"He's so damn ugly, though!" Chanel added.

"I thought so, too," Yolie shrugged. "He draws you in with his superior knowledge of God… He quotes the Bible like a prodigy. He melted me and made love to me for *hours*."

"Wow," Uzenna was surprised. "Well… Look. I need y'all to go over there and choose your apartments. Carla, Isabella, and Jessika will occupy the penthouse units per Joker Red. But all of you need to know that more girls will come so don't be surprised when called on to take a roommate."

"What about our kids?" Jada asked.

"As soon as we get these units furnished with the basics, go get your kids," Uzenna told them.

It took all week to get everything done but with 28 determined women to pitch in, a lot was accomplished. Not only that but an army of decorators, deliverymen from Amazon, Instacart, Walmart, Grubhub, Uber Eats, DoorDash, Wayfair, and many others came through to deliver orders.

By the time Saturday arrived Coral had helped 16 of the ladies reserve flights to their respective states to retrieve their children. All of them left in Uber or Lyft rides. The 10 women that stayed behind were Rosa, Nellie, Yolie, Patricia, MacKenzie, Esmeralda, Lexie, and the three Italian standouts: Carla, Isabella, and Jessika.

The shrill ring of her cell phone jolted Uzenna out of a good afternoon sleep she was having with Coral cuddled up behind her in the penthouse on Sunday. *"Hello?"* She answered tiredly.

"Hey mommie," Joker greeted her. *"You sleep?"*

She smiled. *"Was, but it's okay."*

"You done yet?"

"Our place is dope," she reported.

"I'm sending the girls out," he told her. Uzenna was puzzled. *"Why? I thought you -- the plan was for me to establish a base here and we have the babies in New York. Our midwives are there."*

"Calm down… don't you think I know that? Iani and Brittani already arranged for the midwives to live nearby so they're comin' too."

Uzenna sighed. *"Okay."*

"The boys are on the way," he added. *"All our vehicles are bein' driven out there as we speak."*

"This is all a really, really big move," she worried. *"I mean... Wow. All the money we layin' down. EIE new soldiers... All the girls. We bought our own apartment* **complex**.*"*

"You worry too much," he laughed. *"It's an* **empire**. *An empire needs employees and security forces. Lemme do the worryin'."*

"When will you be here?"

"Very soon."

They ended the call moments later.

CHAPTER TWENTY-FOUR

Joker drove up to the Otisville ranch house to meet with Meth Man Ace. The two men embraced immediately and Ace led Joker into the living room where four Latina women were relaxing in pajamas and bathrobes. Joker knew that Ace had been training his own team of crystal meth makers period from what Ace had told him, the girls were prolific at it which pleased Joker greatly.

"These are the *chicas*," Joker sat down in a comfortable brown leather recliner.

"That's them," Ace acknowledged. "Blanca, Bambina or Bambi… Natalya and Alejandra. All of them are Dominicans."

"Ola chicas," Joker said. "I need y'all to close it out here and move to an obscure base in Illinois."

"How soon?" Ace asked.

"Yesterday."

"What'll happen to all this?"

"Sellin' it off. Time to move on to bigger and better."

———

The Tribeca Loft
New York, NY
Monday, Night

Joker used a key to walk into the beautifully and completely decorated home. He smelled incense and spicy Indian food cooking. Tithi, hearing him enter, came out of the kitchen wearing a fabulous white silk nightgown by La Perla. Her long black hair was pulled back and held in place with the white clamp. She rushed into his arms and he wrapped her body up close against him.

"I'm so happy to see you!" She gushed.

"Me too, baby!" He said and kissed her sweet, soft lip-glossed lips. "Damn... You taste so sweet, India."

They stood there and kissed for untold amount of minutes before she had to break free of him.

"You electrify my brain particles!" She laughed as she walked back into the kitchen. "I'll burn dinner."

"Smells good," he complimented her as he went in behind her to smell it.

"Steaks and rice with a homemade red sauce we make in India," Tithi said, picking up a plate. "Have a seat and let me serve you."

Soon, they were sitting down having a candle light dinner in the dining area. She had a chilled Bordeaux ready as well. This girl was in a class by herself and he *loved* her.

"You gonna spoil me, Tithi." Joker tasted the wine. "This is good. All of it."

"I sent all of the gold my... *intended* had gifted me with," she revealed. "I mailed it to him last week."

Joker looked at her. "That must've been tough."

She nodded. "I knew he'd wanted me for his wife but I never felt anything for him. Just... obligation as my father's daughter."

"Now they all know?"

She nodded affirmatively. "My father and mother called screaming at me."

He took her by the hand after their meal and they sat together on the left seat in the bedroom.

"So, what are we looking at here?" He inquired.

"I need to stay in the U.S.," she said. "I can't go back there. I don't wanna go back."

"Hey," Joker nudged her. "You won't go back there. In fact..." he said, pulling out his cell phone, "I'm texting Mecca Montecristo right now *to please locate and retain INS lawyer in New York for my medical student girlfriend – a foreign exchange student on visa who wishes to become U.S. citizen upon her graduation this fall.* Send me the bill how's that?"

She beamed happily.

They hugged and kissed each other with renewed passion and vigor. He grabbed her ponytail and sucked all over her neck, inhaling her sweets and whispering his love for her in her ear.

Joker picked her up in his powerful arms and carried her to the master bedroom. He stripped out of his clothes as she pulled the covers down and placed large towels across the sheet, in anticipation of preventing the bed linen from getting soiled with sex juices.

Tithi let the La Perla nightgown slip down her lithe cinnamon-colored body until it pooled around her feet. Then she slipped into the bed, her eyes on his engorged penis. To tease him, she turned on to her stomach and opened up her legs, presenting her bare, wet pussy to him. He needed no further prompting.

He had been gentle with her because she was brand new to sex. But tonight, he would break her in right. She turned back around, on her back now, and Joker climbed slowly on top of her and slid that huge dick straight home into her aching little pussy. She gasped and moaned deep in her throat, surprised that he rammed into her so deeply, so fast. But it felt fantastic. He pushed his pole all the way in until she felt its tip mashed into her cervix.

"Look at me, my Indian love," he whispered as he pulled nearly all the way out of her. "I'm in love with you... *I love this wet little pussy of yours. Say it's mine.*"

"This pussy is yours!" She gasped as he slammed it firmly back inside of her. "Ohh!"

Slap! Slap! Slap! Slap! Slap! Sound of his balls on her asshole and ass cheeks made her cry out with ecstasy. The hard and fast strokes he pounded her with made a liquid heat gather at the center of her being where familiar waves of pleasure washed from her uterus up to her back, arms, and legs. He put her little feet up onto his shoulders and pushed her legs all the way up to where her knees nearly touched her shoulders. Then he long-dicked the shit out of her tight "red snapper" pussy.

"On your hands and knees," he commanded her.

Shaking with sexual excitement, Tithi did as she was told. "Please," she begged. "Fuck me!"

Joker showed her no mercy. He slammed right back inside of her as he gripped two handfuls of her sweaty butt cheeks. His entire body was shiny with perspiration. He fucked her like a prize stud would a mare and he had the horse dick to match. He watched her tiny hairless anus squeezed tightly and used their juices to massage it. With a few more long strokes of his big cock, she felt all the tension inside of her explode and dissolved into shutters of an orgasm, leaving her limp and gasping with satisfaction.

While Tithi was trying to catch her breath to regain control, Joker kept pounding into her. She knew if she didn't stop him soon he'd have her screaming so loud that the neighbors might hear. So she forced herself to pull away from him, her pussy dripping.

She turned to face him with her hand over her swollen pussy. She was wide-eyed, her nipples were elongated, and she had the urge to taste him.

"Your cum is all over my dick..."

She went to her knees and grabbed his penis. It was so wet with their juices she could smell her own sex on him. She licked that gorgeous cockhead, running her tongue gently around the thick rim. She wanted to savor him, licking and tasting slowly, but her desire and his need were too great. She swallowed several inches of him, feeling him grow even harder as she tried to take him even deeper into her mouth. She could taste his salty-sweet pre-cum, and it made her crazy for more.

The sound of his breathing increased. She sucked faster, sliding her mouth up and down the length of him. He was moaning, pressing himself in and out of her drooling mouth. As she sucked him, Tithi rubbed her tongue vigorously back and forth along the bottom of his cock. With the thrill she heard him whisper, "I'm cummin'!"

She heard him groan as he spurted three quick shots of hot cum into her mouth. The first went directly in her throat. The second hit the back of her mouth. The third, most tantalizing, lay on her tongue. She swallowed slowly, savoring the taste of him.

Joker collapsed alongside her and watched her finished swallowing his cum. She got up, went to pee, and returned with a hot washcloth. She wiped him down and kissed him. She got up once more to go to the kitchen and did not return for fifteen minutes.

"Had to wash the dishes," she admitted when she came back, still naked. "I'm obsessed with cleaning rather here or at my job or school."

"My wife wants me to share you with her and the other girls," he revealed from nowhere.

She paused as she slipped in the bed beside him. "I knew about the wife... Maybe a side chick or two period... But 'others'?"

Joker pulled out his cell phone and accessed all the photos of his thirteen women. He started talking from the beginning and left out everything that had to do with murder. She let him speak freely...

"Please, don't ask how or what I had to do to free them," he pleaded. "I don't want to lie to you..."

She was stunned. "So, you're the leader of a criminal drug empire... With *thirteen* babies on the way?"

He nodded, hoping he didn't make a mistake telling her all this. He'd hate to run her off or make her fearful.

"Thirteen babies," she repeated, trying to wrap her head around it. "How do you do it? I mean, how does *one man* have the stamina to please and impregnate so many females?"

"Nature and God has blessed me," he shrugged.

"Do you *truly* love me?"

"Do you believe that I do?"

Tithi had tears in her eyes. "I really do. I'm so in love with you!"

"And me with you," he told her. "I'm not a liar. One thing you can count on with me is that I cherish my word."

"So all these girls..." She trailed off. "They *love* you? Your wife *loves* you?"

He nodded. "They all had their names changed to my last name so we can all be one solid family."

"Do they all..." She asked shyly.

"What?"

"You know."

"Have sex with each other?" He asked.

She nodded.

"They all love each other," he explained. "To make it through the darkest of days, they turn to each other for love. For lust. For everything. I showed Uzenna a photo of you while I sucked her pussy... She came so hard, she bruised my lips."

"Which one is she again?"

He pulled up a sexy photo of Uzenna.

"She's beautiful."

"Her skin is the color of honey," he said.

"Are you in a sex cult?" She wanted to know.

"Not at all." he assured her.

"Hypothetically speaking," she stated. "Would they all accept the fact that you and I have a relationship or would they feel threatened?"

"I believe if you gave it a chance, they'd adore you," he told her. "Uzenna is barely twenty years old but she's the leader out of all of them. What she says, or does, they all follow. She gave me permission to pursue you."

Tithi got on top of him and he held her close and tight. Joker really and truly loved this girl and he could tell that she loved him.

"I see now," she whispered.

"See what?"

"Uzenna knew, like I know, that to really have you and keep you, she had to share you with other girls she loved. For them to produce your children and you all be one commune."

They melted into a passionate kiss.

"Is she too sore?" He asked as he palmed her ass and ran his finger down her crack, across her anus, and over her wet pussy lips. "This little Indian pussycat?"

"She's purring."

He was rock hard again. She impaled herself down onto him. This time she rode him slowly until her clitoris went berserk with tingling feelings that sent her galloping to an all-star finish. He flipped her over into the missionary position and gave her a profound grinding.

"I want your cum inside me!" Tithi whispered and gyrated her pussy in tight little circles.

Joker pile drove into her like a porno king and spilled thick jets of his warm semen deep into her cervix. She bit him and licked the sweat from his neck.

"So, good, my king," she breathed. "Sooo goood."

Later on that night he told her, "I'll be in Chicago but I want you there with me. At any time you can break free – even if it's only twenty-four hours – you'll have a charted luxury jet awaiting."

"You spend a lot of money! My God!" She exclaimed. "I can take a bus."

He laughed. "And technically, you can walk or ride a bike, too ... Listen. I have a few million put away. But in Amerikkka you can have one hundred million. If you can't show where you made it at, then you can't spend it. So, I just made a deal with some other bigger, badder, bad guys that have *legit* business connections. I'm looking to be a good guy one day. Anyway, the legit connection will allow me to borrow money from a bank or *banks* with fifty to seventy-five million dollars."

Her mouth dropped open and stayed that way for a full minute. "Oh – my – God!"

"That's right," he said. "I'm investin' it so I can pay it back... Also, so I can pay off all my other debt. So, don't worry about my spending. You have a tablet or cell phone with a to do list or somethin' I can type on?"

She got up and put on a robe, then went to her desk in the corner. She returned two seconds later with a new laptop.

"Number one, call Mecca Montecristo for INS lawyer referral," he typed in. "Two: contact Gulfstream or Lear Jet for luxury flight hours. Three: buy a car... Meanwhile, until we get you something suitable, get a stable rental and a limousine service."

She accepted that. "I hate driving in Manhattan. It's no better than Mumbai. Having a driver at my beck and call I'll like."

"Number Four: Chicago house or apartment," he wrote. He called *Amerikkkan Express/Black Centurion.* "I'm putting you on this account. It's an exclusive card with a lot of power, a lot of reach. Pay the lawyer with it, the Gulfstream account, the car, the Chicago home, your college debt. That's Number Five: pay off college debt. Number Six: pay off your families debts."

She was stunned. "How do I..?"

"Call your father and *ask,*" he advised. "Assert your allegiance to your family but control your own independence. Do you belong to that Hindu temple in your country?"

"Of course," she nodded.

"Set up monthly donations or offerings to be taken from the

card," he said. "That's Number Seven: offering of five hundred dollars month to Hindu temple in India and the same to Hindu temple in New York."

"Thank you, thank you, thank you!" She stated with huge smiles and kisses.

"Number Eight: Gold chains, bracelets, necklaces, rings, earrings, toe rings, ankle bracelets, and waist chains," he told her. "Don't want you wearing it all over New York or Chicago... You'll be robbed. But you're a goddess and look hot in gold. Number Nine: wardrobe. You're a trendy young Indian chick. I want you to have all the top of the line fashion. Prada, Gucci, Manolo Blahniks, Louis Vuitton, La Perla... five hundred dollar panties. And whatever else you need, get."

He later put his hand against her soft warm bosom and slept the most peaceful sleep ever. She rubbed his forehead, temples, and shoulders while staring at him in amazement. She knew he was a millionaire drug kingpin... With a very sexy wife and twelve other beautiful women who were all *pregnant*! But, strangely enough, she felt even more attracted to him and the *oh so sweet and lustful* sexual possibilities that were in store for her. *His wife wants to have sex with me!* She silently squirmed at the thought! *Wow, how many mornings can one man make a woman?*

She felt her pussy pulsing and her clitoris throbbing once again. His sperm was still swimming inside of her and streaming out of her anus. As she touched her vagina she fantasized about carrying his baby and it was that thought that she went to sleep with beside him.

CHAPTER TWENTY-FIVE

The "Twin Towers" War Room
Chicago, IL
Thursday 6:00

"Okay here we go..." Joker stated as he and Ghostman used thumbtacks to secure two Chicago street maps to the wall.

They were inside of one of the apartments of the "Twin Towers" apartment buildings they had purchased. Joker and Uzenna's penthouse was in the same building where the Chicago War Room was established on the 4th floor. Everyone was there: Boo, Divine, Bushwacker, Black, N9NE, Monk, Caesar, Ground War, Fast Eddie, Broliks, Bible, Chief, Knarf, Rogue, Hard Knox, Bonecrusher, La Colombiana, Breach, A-Son, Mustafa, Goliath, Blaze, Joker, Meth Man, Ghostman, Leah, Diane, Uzenna, and several more newcomers that Joker introduced.

"Before we start," Joker said as he turned to look at the army behind him. "Most of you know our esteemed comrades from the Army: Blackout, Ironhide, Barricade, and Devastator. And from the Air Force: Starscream, Rebel One, Blackbird, Darkstar, and Raptor.

What's poppin' y'all? Welcome to Everything Is Everything – E.I.E."

The new soldiers nodded. Like many of the other EIE soldiers, the newcomers were freelance contractors for various private military companies (PMC's). Joker only allowed those he *knew* or trusted most to join his ranks. And all EIE dealt with were killers, men and women, who were verified and the masters of their craft. For instance, Joker loved the lasting previous surge of newcomers because they came equally matched with the rest of his EIE soldiers, especially when it came to "mercenary" or military experience.

They were not only combat soldiers but they had the knowledge to monitor advanced weapons, military weapons, rendering technical assistance, and providing logistical support. In fact, it was Blackout, Breach, and Barricade who'd use their contracts in the RAF or British Royal Air Force to obtain some high-tech communications equipment needed for the Chicago job.

"The Chicago eighty or simply put C-8," Joker called it. "We have a mighty, mighty job ahead of us. There are eighty targets that we need to neutralize."

Ghostman stood up and used a red laser to point at the 50-inch monitors on the wall opposite from where they all sat on sofas and chairs in the living area.

"Do the clickin' for me, Lee," Ghost said to Leah.

She put the first two neighborhoods onto the big screens.

"First, we have to focus on West Garfield Park and Englewood," Ghostman explained. "We have three of the United States' highest ranking Latin Kings in there. Each of them are plugged into *Los Aztecas*. What's the significance? Well, the Los Aztecas work with the Juarez Cartel and Los Zetas who run drugs, smuggle illegal aliens, and kill consulate officials. The Aztecas are a powerful paramilitary force on both sides of the Mexico border. They have military structure that helps them keep order. So, we have to understand our enemy here. These cats are the real deal."

Uzenna, Diane, Joker, and Meth Man Ace passed out a stack of photographs. Leah posted the first photograph of a Puerto Rican man onto both screens.

"They call him *'El Verdugo'* which means what Colombiana?" Ghostman asked her.

"*The Executioner,*" She translated.

Ghostman pointed at the big screens. "This character, whose birth name is Alberto Huerta Moreno, is the number one assassin and smuggler for their Juarez Cartel. He's rumored to have killed and tortured approximately thirty men and women between Chicago, L.A., and Mexico for the Juarez Cartel. In 2018 he was tried for a triple murder in Chicago and was acquitted, to everyone's shock. Ask me why they call him The Executioner?"

"Why, nigga?" A-Son asked him.

Ghostman turned to Leah. "Lee..."

Leah posted several pictures of decapitated bodies with obvious signs of what could only be described as *obscene* or *extreme* torture to the dead. Fingers were missing. Penises severed. Penises brutalized with some sort of hot poker or searing device. Breasts cut off.

Now the EIE killers were angry.

"This," Ghost emphasized to A-Son, "*This* is why, my nigga."

There was complete silence in the room.

"Most of us are thinkin'... *oh, okay, he's one man,*" Joker interjected. "*We've taken down worse... Who? When?*"

"ISIS is way worse," Black N9NE mentioned.

"I agree," said Bushwacker. "Most of them we took out with air support, full on assaults with a hundred men in our units, and −"

"Snipers takin' out their leadership," Monk added.

"Bingo," Joker commented. "Here, we have no air support, we operate *illegally* where *we're* the fuckin' bad guys... And this Executioner has his own army out there. Make no doubt about it, we are on their turf and we can't go in with hundred-man hit team. They *own* West Garfield Park and Englewood which means if we go in and expose our hand… We most likely will get trapped inside of these extremely dangerous Chicago neighborhoods."

Silence all around.

"If the Aztecas aren't bad enough… Leah?" Ghost spoke back up. "Let's look at these Mara Salvatrucha or MS-13 members: Marco Antonio Pineda AKA *Chucho* and Francisco Hernandez Garcia AKA *El Taliban*. Both of these bastards are from the Los Zetas Cartel. Our intelligence reports has *twenty-two* of them who cover Englewood and protect Chucho and Taliban with their *lives*."

"Aight," A-Son sighed. "So we see… getting' inside this dense urban terrain won't be the problem… getting' *out* after the hit, that's the problem."

Ghostman nodded. "Yeah… We have to say it: some of us will not be returning."

"And we got eighty of these mufuckas to hit?" Fast Eddie stated, exasperation dripping from his voice.

Everybody felt the same way.

"These are the worst of the worst," Joker said, pulling up a chair to sit in front of everyone. "It gets a little easier after these…"

"You and Ghostman are highlighting all this doom and gloom in the forecast, Daddy," Uzenna blurted out. "Why not talk about a strategy that will bring 'em all back alive?"

"I was getting to that," Joker informed her and turned back to the group. "There is one way… It's a radical strategy but desperate times call for desperate measures."

He had everyone's undivided attention.

"Okay," Ground War stated. "Spit it out, nigga."

"OPERATION BLUE CONDOR," Joker revealed to them. "We throw the city into a chaos it hasn't seen since *Prohibition* and Al Capone. And we start a war… not our own. But an unexpected war Against unsuspecting foes… the Aztecas, MS-13, and Los Zetas versus Chicago's Finest."

He let that sink in for a second.

"How we s'posed to do that?" Caesar inquired.

Joker had a cold blooded, ruthless expression on his face. "We're gonna plant ourselves within the bowels of West Garfield Park and Englewood and wait for a CPD Lieutenant or captain to drive through and take the shot that will be heard around the world. And then, after that shot, we blow to smithereens three more cop cars as they respond to the scene."

The group of soldiers were loudly cheering on that plan because they knew what it meant.

A bloody war was on the way to the City of Chicago. And it's code name was: OPERATION BLUE CONDOR...

To be continued:

Hittaz 3

Coming Soon...

OTHER BOOKS BY

URBAN AINT DEAD

Tales 4rm Da Dale

By **Elijah R. Freeman**

The Hottest Summer Ever

By **Elijah R. Freeman**

Despite The Odds

By **Juhnell Morgan**

The Swipe 1

By **Toola**

Good Girl Gone Rouge

By **Manny Black**

Hittaz 1

By **Lou Garden Price, Sr**

BOOKS BY URBAN AINT DEAD'S C.E.O

Elijah R. Freeman

Triggadale 1, 2 & 3

Tales 4rm Da Dale

The Hottest Summer Ever

Murda Was The Case 1 & 2

Follow

Elijah R. Freeman

On Social Media

FB: Elijah R. Freeman

IG: @the_future_of_urban_fiction